NO HOLDS BARRED

The cougar's weight knocked Fargo to the ground. Together they tumbled down the mountainside. Bracing himself on the incline, Fargo grabbed the cougar's throat. The cat dug its claws into Fargo's shoulders, twisting its head violently to wrench free from the big man's choking grip.

Fargo willed himself to ignore the searing pain in his shoulders as he felt sweat pouring from him and his biceps turn rock hard fighting to keep the bared, flesh-ripping teeth from his exposed throat. . . .

The Trailsman was in a wilderness where only the most savage survived—and the cougar was nothing compared to the men who roamed this godforsaken place. . . .

BLAZING NEW TRAILS
WITH SKYE FARGO

☐ **THE TRAILSMAN #107: GUNSMOKE GULCH by Jon Sharpe.** Skye Fargo blasts a white-slaving ring apart and discovers that a beauty named Annie has a clue to a gold mine worth slaying for—a proposition that makes Skye ready to blaze a trail through a gunsmoke screen of lethal lies. (168038—$3.50)

☐ **THE TRAILSMAN #109: LONE STAR LIGHTNING by Jon Sharpe.** Skye Fargo on a Texas manhunt with two deadly weapons—a blazing gun and a fiery female. (168801—$3.50)

☐ **THE TRAILSMAN #110: COUNTERFEIT CARGO by Jon Sharpe.** The pay was too good for Skye Fargo to turn down, so he's guiding a wagon train loaded with evil and heading for hell. (168941—$3.50)

☐ **THE TRAILSMAN #111: BLOOD CANYON by Jon Sharpe.** Kills Fast, the savage Cheyenne medicine man, hated Skye Fargo like poison. And when Skye followed a perverse pair of paleskin fugitives into redskin hands, Kills Fast wasn't about to live up to his name. (169204—$3.50)

☐ **THE TRAILSMAN #112: THE DOOMSDAY WAGONS by Jon Sharpe.** Skye Fargo follows a trail of corpses on a trip through hell for a showdown with marauding redskins. (169425—$3.50)

☐ **THE TRAILSMAN #113: SOUTHERN BELLES by Jon Sharpe.** The Trailsman had plenty of bullets in his gunbelt when a Mississippi paddle-wheeler found itself in a mist of mystery as ripe young beauties were plucked from its cabins. (169635—$3.50)

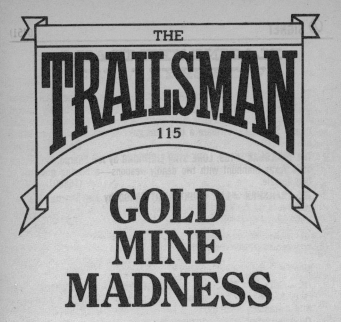

THE
TRAILSMAN
115

GOLD
MINE
MADNESS

by

Jon Sharpe

Ⓢ
A SIGNET BOOK

SIGNET
Published by the Penguin Group
Penguin Books USA Inc., 375 Hudson Street,
New York, New York 10014, U.S.A.
Penguin Books Ltd, 27 Wrights Lane,
London W8 5TZ, England
Penguin Books Australia Ltd, Ringwood,
Victoria, Australia
Penguin Books Canada Ltd, 10 Alcorn Ave., Suite 300,
Toronto, Canada M4V 3B2
Penguin Books (N.Z.) Ltd, 182-190 Wairau Road,
Auckland 10, New Zealand

Penguin Books Ltd, Registered Offices:
Harmondsworth, Middlesex, England

First published by Signet, an imprint of New American Library,
a division of Penguin Books USA Inc.

First Printing, July, 1991
10 9 8 7 6 5 4 3 2 1

The first chapter of this book originally appeared in *The Tamarind Trail,*
the one hundred fourteenth volume in this series.

 REGISTERED TRADEMARK—MARCA REGISTRADA

Printed in the United States of America

PUBLISHER'S NOTE
This is a work of fiction. Names, characters, places, and incidents either
are the product of the author's imagination or are used fictitiously, and any
resemblance to actual persons, living or dead, events, or locales is entirely
coincidental.

The Trailsman

Beginnings ... they bend the tree and they mark the man. Skye Fargo was born when he was eighteen. Terror was his midwife, vengeance his first cry. Killing spawned Skye Fargo, ruthless, cold-blooded murder. Out of the acrid smoke of gunpowder still hanging in the air, he rose, cried out a promise never forgotten.

The Trailsman they began to call him all across the West: searcher, scout, hunter, the man who could see where others only looked, his skills for hire but not his soul, the man who lived each day to the fullest, yet trailed each tomorrow. Skye Fargo, the Trailsman, the seeker who could take the wildness of a land and the wanting of a woman and make them his own.

Autumn, 1860, the Colorado Territory,
when quaking aspen turned golden
and a trek through the mountains
promised mystery and danger
at every turn . . .

1

The big man astride the magnificent black-and-white pinto stallion cut his lake-blue eyes to the right and glanced west once more. The thunderheads he had watched build since noon had finally moved over the mountain range into the valley. The still air hung heavy with moisture; not a leaf stirred, not even the quaking aspen.

After all he'd been through of late the prospect of rain represented a welcome relief, although he preferred not to get drenched to the skin. He had fled the young widow's house two days ago and left his poncho behind. The crazy female bedded him on pretense she hadn't slept with a man in over a year, since her late husband died. At the height of their romp, just as both were pounding away, straining for the crescendo, the little bitch asked him to marry her. He scooped up his clothes and ran without looking back.

The soft sounds of the Ovaro's slow-moving hooves mingled with those made by an unseen shallow stream gurgling over a rocky bottom a short distance on his right. A woodpecker started drilling for a worm somewhere off to his left. The stallion's ears perked and swiveled in the direction of the new sound.

The run-in with Widow Brown was a continuation of a series of pretenses that plagued the big man, pretenses that put him on the trail headed south. He loathed the games people played, especially the widows.

It started in the saloon at Royal Flush, Montana, a small gold-mining town. He caught a man cheating in a game of five-card draw. The nimble-fingered fellow made the mistake of drawing down on him. The big man shot him dead.

There were other "games" the farther south he drifted. Twice in Wyoming Territory he was approached by females on pretense that they had been beaten by men. Their stories were so convincing that he took pity on the two women. He sought out and confronted the two woman-beaters, beat the shit out of both . . . only to learn the women, in each instance, had lied to him. They were out to get even with the men for rebuking them.

In Grizzly, Colorado, a panic-stricken old man rushed up to him and said he had just been robbed by two men in back of the town's saloon. The old man led him behind the saloon, where the duo stood taking a leak, counting money. The big man didn't ask any questions. He proceeded to beat both to a bloody pulp. He subsequently learned they were counting poker winnings. By that time the old man was long gone with the money.

The widow's game followed two days later.

He glanced west again, wondered if his run of bad luck was over, the promise of an October storm in the high country notwithstanding. The big man sure as hell hoped so.

Powderhorn, his immediate destination, came into view. He saw the little mining hamlet had grown since he last visited it. Back then, only two structures stood: a trading post and next to it a saloon. Both had been shabby then and were even more so now. Silas "Beaver" Trapp built the log and sod-roof trading post, the original structure. When gold was discovered nearby,

Miss Comely built the Powderhorn Saloon. Miners named the village after Miss Comely's saloon, which gave them so much pleasure.

Coming closer, he now saw a land and assayer's office had been erected adjacent to the saloon, and next to it a smithy's shop. Across the street, directly in front of the saloon stood a new bank. To the right of the bank was a small general store, also new. Left of the bank, a spacious two-story house was under construction. The yellow-pine framing was up. A shaft of rapidly disappearing sunlight punched through a gap in the mountains and struck the framing, setting it aglow in golden colors.

Hitching the Ovaro to the rail at the saloon, the big man noticed the lack of activity, and thought it odd. Not a horse, buggy, or wagon stood in front of any of the buildings. At this hour he expected to see and hear the hell-raising, boisterous miners. Were it not for lamplight spilling from the saloon into the street, Powderhorn resembled a ghost town. He reckoned the gold mine had played out and the miners had moved on.

As he stepped onto the saloon's porch, a few huge drops of rain pelted, dimpling the soil behind him.

Out of habit, the big man paused at the double doors to look inside before entering. A brawl might be in the making—or worse, a gunfight. But he saw none of this.

Miss Comely's elderly, shaky bartender, a former gambler who went by the name of Tops, stood behind the bar, cleaning a shot glass. Top's hands shook so much that he dropped it.

Miss Comely rested the small of her back against the bar's edge across from Tops. She talked in low tones with two older men seated at the table, drinks before them.

The big man recognized one of the men: Gold Pan

Jack, a crusty old prospector who had been around for years.

The old fellow occupying the chair across from Gold Pan wore city clothes. The big man reckoned him a business man, or a wandering drummer.

The only other person in the saloon, a terribly skinny female dressed as a saloon girl, clearly Indian, leaned on the bar down aways from Miss Comely. The Indian appeared bored to tears. She stared blankly at the rack of elk horns mounted on the wall behind the bar.

When he pushed through the swinging doors, all five people jumped, as though a shot had been fired, and turned to face him.

Miss Comely recovered first. Smiling hugely, she said excitedly, "Well, bless my soul if it isn't Skye Fargo. C'mere, big man, and let me hug you."

On pull back, she whispered, "God, but you feel good. Long time no see, Fargo." Strengthening her voice, she said to everyone, "We're going to celebrate the Trailsman's return. Drinks are on the house tonight."

"Make mine bourbon," Fargo told Tops. He watched Tops try to fill a glass. The shaky-handed bartender poured about as much on the bartop as he did filling the glass.

Skinny moseyed up to him. Putting an arm around him, she said, as though a long drought was finally over and might come back within seconds, "Want to have some fun? I buck fast and good."

Miss Comely snapped, "Leave him alone, Lay-Me-Down. Shit, the man just got here. Quit playing with him. You hear me, Lay-Me-Down? I said stop grabbing at Fargo."

Censured soundly by the boss-woman, Lay-Me-Down reluctantly let go of him, turned to Tops, and asked for a mug of beer.

"Ain't no beer," Tops told her. "You know it's all gone. The beer wagon ain't come yet."

Miss Comely snorted, "Hunh! Furthermore the beer wagon ain't coming, either. I told them when they brought the last load not to bring any more." She looked at Fargo. "Powderhorn is drying out. This place is going straight to hell. I don't know if I can hold out much longer, waiting for business to pick back up. Shit, it's bad."

"Did the mine play out?" Fargo questioned.

"Hell, no," Gold Pan barked. "That high-tone bitch is to blame."

Fargo glanced at Miss Comely for her to explain. Hurt and anger filled her voice when she said, "Grace Hatfield. Remember that name, Skye Fargo. Stay away from her, if you know what's good for you."

"What the hell happened?" Fargo quizzed, his brow furrowing.

He watched Miss Comely guzzle from a whiskey bottle. Bristling mad, she explained, "Grace came to Powderhorn on her personal crusade to give good morals to the misguided, lost sheep, immoral people living on the frontier. Those were the bitch's very words. Misguided, lost sheep, my ass. The hell of it is, those sorry-assed miners went along with Grace." Miss Comely's hazel eyes filled with tears as she looked into his lake-blues and added most bitterly, "Ever damn one of them got religion. What am I, oh, what am I gonna do, Fargo?"

And that answered that. Fargo had visions of Grace Hatfield being a plump, older woman, a prune-faced, scripture-quoting virgin spinster surrounded by scungy-looking miners bawling their eyes out while listening to her brand of hellfire and brimstone. Fargo did not need or want to hear any of that. He mumbled, "In time, maybe the miners will backslide and fall off the wagon. Most do, you know."

He heard a chorus of relieved sighs escape everyone's lips, then Lay-Me-Down said, "Hope so. I'm getting out of practice."

Fargo looked at her. "Are you Ute? Where did you learn to speak English so well?"

"Yes, I'm Ute," Lay-Me-Down answered. "Beaver taught me."

"By the way, where is Beaver?" Fargo asked.

Gold Pan snorted, "That high-tone female cornered Beaver first cracker out of the barrel. When she started lacing into him, he screamed and hightailed it into the mountains and never came back. I should've gone with him."

"When was that?" Fargo inquired.

"Two months ago," the old gentleman seated opposite of Gold Pan answered.

Fargo stepped to him. Extending his hand, he smiled and said, "I don't believe we've met."

Rising, the older man gripped Fargo's hand. "My name is Samuel B. Quick. I own the bank across the street." He pumped Fargo's hand slowly, as though it were a great effort.

Fargo felt the weak grip. He said, "I noticed a building going up next to your bank. Looked like a big house. Has construction halted till things return to normal?"

Miss Comely answered venomously, "Yet another mark left by the bitch. I invested every cent I had in building a new saloon. Now all my plans are shot to hell." Tears welled in her eyes when she lamented, "I even paid the passage for six French tarts to come over on a boat. Those tarts are due to arrive here any day now. For the life of me, I do not know where I am going to put them. The crew working on my new saloon caught Grace's religion, too, right along with those sorry-assed miners. They said they weren't about to build such a sinful place, laid down their

14

hammers and saws, and walked off the job. Oh, me, Fargo, what am I gonna do?"

He silently agreed that it was indeed a most sad state of affairs. Still, the high-tone woman had a measure of his respect. Anyone who could corral the otherwise loose morals of miners and construction workers had to be reckoned with.

"Where did she come from, anyhow?" Fargo wondered aloud.

"Pascagoula, Mississippi," Quick answered.

After a long silence, Miss Comely sighed heavily, then said, "Well, enough of this kind of talk. We've bared our rotten, misguided souls to Fargo. He probably won't ever meet up with the woman anyhow." Cocking one eyebrow, as though she might have erred, Miss Comely cut her eyes to Fargo's chiseled face and quickly added, "By the way, where are you headed?"

"Reckoned I'd go south for the winter," Fargo began. "See what's happening in Tucson."

"Tucson?" a voice from behind the double doors asked. "Did I hear Tucson?"

They turned as a shapely, young fiery red-haired woman pushed her way inside. She carried a parfleche folder under her left arm, a small wooden box in her hand. A smile blossomed on her face as she looked at Fargo through light-green, inquisitive eyes.

"You heard correct, ma'am," Fargo verified. He noticed the others stared nervously at the woman.

"You here on a crusade, or something?" Miss Comely finally asked. "If you are, we don't want to hear about it."

"No, I don't think so," the redhead replied. "This is the only place in town showing light. I've been on the porch waiting for the rain to stop. My name's Maureen. Maureen Bodner." She stepped between

Fargo and Miss Comely, set her parfleche and box on the bartop, and ordered a beer from Tops.

"Ain't got none," Tops told her.

Eyeing Maureen suspiciously, Miss Comely said, "What's between the rawhide, girlie?"

"And the box, sweetie?" Lay-Me-Down added cutely.

"Rum, then," Maureen told Tops. She glanced at Lay-Me-Down, then at Miss Comely.

"The Powderhorn doesn't stock rum," Miss Comely muttered frostily.

The hairs on Fargo's nape perked and started to tingle. The glances the redhead slid to the saloonkeeper and the Ute might as well have been words that said, You two are trash. And Fargo had also caught Miss Comely's and Lay-Me-Down's sudden change in attitude the moment Maureen walked in. He wondered if the hairs perking warned him a game had started. Subtle though it was, the three female's body language, coupled with the change in inflection they put in their tone of voice, signaled to him a contest was now in progress. He wondered if their game involved him. With my run of bad luck, Fargo decided, it sure as hell appears that way.

Maureen Bodner continued the game. She smiled when she slid a hand down to Fargo's groin and rubbed, saying dryly, "Stuff. What kind of liquor do you have?"

Now he knew for sure he was indeed involved.

Tops answered, "Whiskey, bourbon, and one bottle of gin."

"Stuff?" Lay-Me-Down echoed, a puzzled expression on her red face.

"What stuff?" Miss Comely asked, obviously rankled. She glanced at the parfleche.

Maureen continued to rub as she said, "Pour me a glassful of bourbon. The parfleche holds sheets of

16

sketch paper, the box my pencils and erasers. I'm an artist, capturing scenes on the frontier, sketching colorful characters living on the edge of civilization."

Lay-Me-Down and Miss Comely shot nervous glances to the rubbing hand. Pain laced Miss Comely's tone when she suggested, "Stop doing that to him. He's tired."

At the same time Fargo said, "No, I'm not," Lay-Me-Down offered, "Dog-tired."

Looking at the big man from over the rim of the glass, Maureen stopped rubbing. She took a swallow of bourbon, then said to Fargo, "Please bring my folder." She picked up the glass of bourbon and the box, stepped to the two old men's table. Sitting, she tossed Miss Comely a fleeting smile—a put-down if ever Fargo saw one—and said, "I'm going to draw the big man's portrait."

"Mine next?" Gold Pan asked hopefully.

Maureen reached over and turned Gold Pan's head so she could see it in profile. Cocking her head, she squinted one green eye and studied his pose. "Maybe," she mumbled.

"Where do you want me?" Fargo asked.

"Sit across from me so we can share the same light. Would somebody bring a lamp over here?"

Miss Comely and the Ute didn't budge one inch. They didn't have to; the banker and prospector pushed and shoved each other to capture the lamp.

All watched Maureen remove a sheet of drawing paper from the folder and open the box. Then she told Fargo to lean in a tad and fold his arms at the elbows on top of the table. Then she told him to slowly turn his head to the left until she said stop. Having posed him, she started sketching.

Miss Comely's and Lay-Me-Down's curiosity got the better of them. They drifted to the table, had a look-see at the sketch, and made bitchy comments about the accuracy of Maureen's work. "Not enough chisel to his face," Miss Comely grunted.

"Yeah, and you drawed his nose too small," Lay-Me-Down complained.

"Looks just like the Trailsman to me," Gold Pan corrected.

Maureen asked the banker, "What do you think, Mr. Quick? A tad of highlight on the nose?"

"Maybe. Just a tad, though," Quick agreed.

After about thirty minutes, Maureen declared Fargo's portrait finished. She went to the bar to get a refill of Tops' bourbon while the others moved around the table to get a better look at the portrait. Miss Comely said it didn't look anything like Fargo. Gold Pan snorted it did, too, look exactly like Fargo. Quick commented she had even drawn the fly that lit on Fargo's shoulder. Fargo said he liked it.

Maureen came back to the table and signed her name on the portrait, printed: POWDERHORN SALOON, MISS COMELY, PROPRIETOR; and dated it SEPT 27, 1860. She glanced up at Fargo and asked, "What did Jack call you? The Trailsman?"

Fargo and Gold Pan nodded.

"What might the Trailsman be?" Maureen inquired.

"A mean bastard." Miss Comely chuckled.

"Then I'll title the portrait, Skye Fargo, The Trailsman."

They watched her print the words just below his portrait.

Miss Comely picked it up, turned the portrait to the lamplight, smiled, and said, "Girlie, I owe you for mentioning the saloon and my name. What can I give you in return for doing such a nice thing?"

Maureen replied faster than a striking diamondback, "Give me and Fargo a bed to use for a little while."

"You got it," Miss Comely said flatly. "You can use mine. It's already broke in."

"Aw, I missed out again," Lay-Me-Down muttered as she moved to the bar.

"Where is your bed?" Maureen asked. She closed the lid on the box, tucked the portrait inside the parfleche, then stood.

"Fargo will show you," Miss Comely said.

Apparently I don't have any say in the matter, Fargo thought. He stepped to the double doors.

"Where are you going, Fargo?" Maureen gasped. She hurried to stop him.

Fargo looked at her and nodded toward the street. "Don't get nervous, honey. I'm just checking the weather."

"You scared me," Maureen murmured. She clutched his arm, but did not try to pull him away from the doors.

Unspoken though it was, Fargo reckoned he'd made his point. No verbal point was required. Action spoke louder than words. All it took to stop the bullshit was for him to head for the doors. He didn't know what he would have done if she had called his bluff. Rain was coming down by bucketsfull. Fargo had no intention of getting soaked to the skin. Not when there was a perfectly sound and dry bed in the back room. Still, Maureen and the others had to hear it. Fargo said, "Don't ever take me for granted unless somebody is trying to kill you. Then you can count on my help." He shot the redhead a wink and they left the room.

Miss Comely's room and the iron bed in it were a pure mess. Clothes were strewn on the floor, hanging out of bureau drawers, draped over the headboard, and the sheets on the bed were twisted and rumpled beyond recognition. Only one pillow, Miss Comely's threadbare red velvet rump pillow, lay on the bed. The two regular, goose-down pillows lay where she had thrown them on the floor. Oddly, the straight-back chair stood clean as a whistle. Fargo thought the room was perfect for Maureen's and his immediate needs. He closed the door.

The artist couldn't wait for the bed, him or her to undress. Nimble fingers opened his fly as she dropped to her knees. Maureen gasped when she pulled his swelling length out of his fly.

Fargo felt her lips tighten around the mushroomlike ruby-red crown and draw the foreskin down. A hot tongue caressed the blood-swollen bulb momentarily, then licked downward. He heard her gulping and gurgling on his throbbing shaft as she took in more and more of it. He pulled her head back. Her lips were drawn so tight they smacked when he came out.

Maureen cast an excited glance up at him.

He pulled her to her feet, saying, "Undress, then put your shapely ass on that rump pillow." He sat in the straight-back to take off his boots.

Maureen stood next to the bureau to quickly shed her clothes. She stood naked before Fargo could pull off the second boot. Gazing at her fiery-hot, bushy patch, he wondered if he was about to enter the gateway to Grace Hatfield's perception of hell. He lifted his gaze to her bosom. Tiny nipples, hardly larger than his own, protruded proudlike from quarter-sized areolae. The breasts, perfectly symmetrical, were milk-white, flecked with freckles, and about the size of small cantaloupes, and just as firm.

The redhead knew how to tease, arouse and excite a man all right, Fargo thought, slipping his Levi's off. He said, "Hop on the bed. Do what I told you."

Maureen was fast to obey. She tucked the pillow under her rump, spread her legs wide, and purred a promise. "Big man, I'm going to give you the wildest ride you ever had."

He believed she would damn sure try. Maureen had all the equipment to do just that. Fargo took one final look at the gates to hell, stood, and moved to the bed.

Maureen greeted him with open arms and legs. He got between the legs and started on the breasts first. Fargo, too, know how to tease, arouse, and excite a woman. He nibbled on the nipples, kissed the areolae, love-bit the pillowy breasts before capturing all he could in his mouth.

Maureen trembled, arched her back, and gasped, "Jesus . . . that feels so good. Suck harder . . . bite them. Oh, Jesus, Jesus . . . yes, yes, that's it." She began squirming, arching higher and higher. Her left hand went to his head and pressed hard, encouraging him to take in more, while her right hand gripped his hard-on and stroked.

After one final rolling of the tiny, rock-hard nipples between his teeth, Fargo moved into position to find out whether or not the hellcat under him could fulfill her promise.

Her hand moved from his rock-hard, elongated prod to her blood-swollen lower lips and parted them. She moaned, "Take me, Fargo. Oh, yes, take me." She positioned his summit for entry.

Fargo felt the slick opening accept the head. Maureen wanted more than that; she shoved up. Fargo went in about halfway. Moaning joyously, she raised her hips, then her legs, and locked her ankles on his hard buttocks. Fargo thrust all the way in the hot tunnel.

She gasped through gritted teeth, "Aaagh! Uhmm! So long, so big. I didn't expect . . . Oh, Jesus . . . you're so big."

He felt her heels dig in, her fingernails rake his back. Fargo began gyrating and pumping. Her hips rose even higher and she started bucking, gasping loudly. Soon the semicontrolled thrusts and upward shoves, gyrating, and writhing gave way to wild abandon. He thrust pistonlike inside an undersize cylinder.

Both of them were bathed with sweat, their bodies made slapping sounds as they met and pounded.

Fargo felt her first of several contractions seize around his organ.

Lightning flashed on the windowpane. Thunder rumbled into Powderhorn. A fierce wind blew. Hail started pelting the roof.

Four things happened simultaneously: the hellcat screamed, "I'm coming!"; a massive bolt of lightning struck a tree a short distance from the window; Fargo erupted; and a mighty explosion knocked out the windowpane and shook the entire saloon.

Fargo knew at once the bolt of lightning didn't trigger the loud sound. Neither was it caused by thunder.

No, the explosion was manmade.

Both men listened to the falling shingles. Fargo often made slapping sounds as they met and produced Fargo felt her first of several contractions seize around his organ.

Lightning flashed on the washbasins. Fragile

2

Before the saloon stopped shaking, Fargo was pulling up his Levi's, listening to Miss Comely and Lay-Me-Down scream. Bare-chested and barefoot, the big man swung his gun belt around his hips and headed for the door. Maureen slipped into her pantaloons and followed him.

The blast had blown the windowpanes inward. Quick and Gold Pan lay covered by shattered glass. They had caught the brunt of the explosion. Quick mumbled incoherently.

Miss Comely and the Ute had also been knocked to the floor. As the saloonkeeper reached for the lip of the bar, she shook her head to clear it. Lay-Me-Down had made it to her knees. She, too, shook her head.

Sprinting past the two females, Fargo glimpsed Tops' shaky hands rise from behind the bar and grab its rim.

Fargo rushed to the front porch. Howling wind and sheets of rain greeted him. He was soaked to the skin within seconds. Thunder rumbled, lightning flashed. Through all of it he saw flames licking from the rear of the bank. The bank leaned against the new structure. Most of its roof littered the street. A large section lay smoking. Fargo knew at once what had happened.

Maureen, then Miss Comely and Gold Pan Jack

appeared next to him. "Quick's bank?" Gold Pan asked.

"Yes," Fargo answered. "It's been robbed. Get the banker. Bring him out here."

"Nothing like this has ever happened before," Miss Comely observed. "Are you going after the robbers?"

"In this weather?" Fargo shot back. "No. It wouldn't do any good. Their tracks are being washed over as fast as they are laid down."

Quick and Gold Pan pushed through the double doors. Quick gasped, "Oh, my God!"

"How much money did you have, Mr. Quick?" Fargo quizzed.

Quick rubbed his jaw, muttered, "Three thousand in cash. Twenty thousand in gold."

"Let's go check," Fargo suggested. He stepped off the porch, headed toward the bank.

Everyone except Tops followed him. The front door and windows beside it had been blown out. Fargo jerked the buckled door off its hinges and went inside. Lightning flashed. He saw the wall containing the teller's cage had been blown to smithereens.

Quick gasped, "Oh, my God! I'm ruined."

"Your bank sure is," Gold Pan agreed.

"Where was the money and gold?" Fargo questioned.

"I'll show you," Quick replied. He stepped around Fargo and began threading his way around and over smoldering debris. Following in Quick's footsteps, Fargo saw the entire back wall of the bank had been torn away by the blast. The back wall of the bank was also the back wall of the vault. It was missing, of course. The wall surrounding the heavy steel vault door lay splintered on the floor. Oddly, the vault door itself stood intact. Quick stepped around it.

Fargo and the others watched the banker search for and find a large strongbox in the debris. The lock had been pried open. Quick raised the lid open. The box was empty. "Gone," Quick half-shouted. "All of the cash is gone."

Fargo glanced around for the gold. "Where did you keep the precious metal?"

"In the woodbin," Quick answered. "Two bags under the wood." He pointed at the bin built into a standing wall.

Gold Pan went to the bin with Fargo. The two men started emptying the bin. Gold Pan pulled one of the bags out, Fargo the other. Gold Pan opened his, looked inside, then said, "You're a lucky bastard, Quick. Looks like it's all here."

Fargo handed his bag to the banker, then went behind the bank and scanned for signs on the ground. But it was too dark and muddy for him to make out anything. He suggested that everyone return to the saloon.

Back in the Powderhorn, they found Tops stoking a fire in the hearth. He had swept the glass over into one corner and covered the windows with blankets to keep out the wind and rain. The women hurried to the fireplace and put their backs to it. Gold Pan and Quick set the bags of gold on the bar. Fargo went behind the bar and poured each a shot of whiskey to knock off the cold of night. He took the remainder to the women.

After taking a swig, Miss Comely suggested a sleeping arrangement. "Seeing how's there are only two beds, mine and Lay-Me-Down's, and seven of us, why—"

"I'll sleep out here," Tops interrupted.

"Six of us," Miss Comely corrected, "why don't me and girlie here cuddle with Fargo. Gold Pan and Quick can sleep with Skinny butt."

"Take off your clothes, " Tops began. "I'll hang 'em on backs of chairs to dry."

Lay-Me-Down and Maureen had a contest to see who could undress the fastest. Fargo declared it a tie. He told Miss Comely and Maureen to go warm his bed, that he'd join them in a few minutes. Quick and Gold Pan shucked their clothes and laid them on the bar. The Ute led them to her room.

While Tops spread the clothing before the fire, Fargo ambled behind the bar and helped himself to a glass of bourbon. After taking a sip, he asked Tops, "Any strangers in town?"

"Only that woman that drew your picture."

"When did she arrive? Ever see her before?"

"No. I saw her at the same time you did. Are you thinking she had something to do with the robbery?"

"Don't rightly know. I want to say no."

"Well, Fargo, she was in bed with you at the time."

Fargo nodded. "That she was." He moved to stand with his back to the fire. "I remember watching a magician perform in Seattle. A pretty, scantily dressed young woman assisted him. Handed him the black top hat, took away his black cape, and so forth. He showed us the inside of that hat—it was empty, of course—then jerked a rabbit out of it. He did other magical things, too. Like cutting a newspaper into ribbons, wadded it up, then he opened his hands and out floated the same sheet of paper in one piece. He did other things, too, like making scantily dressed young women disappear in a puff of yellow smoke.

"I went to him after the performance and asked if I could buy him a drink. He took me up on the offer. So we drank until he got light-headed. I asked how he did it, meaning the magic, because I had kept my eyes on his hands all the time."

"What did he say?"

"He said it was an illusion. He made us think it was on the up and up when it really wasn't."

"Back in my gambling days, before I took to shaking, I had steady hands, nimble fingers. I could do the same thing right before a card player's very own eyes. But we didn't call it an illusion. We called it cheating."

Fargo nodded. "I guess what I'm saying is, what if she, the artist, was his assistant."

"Uh, I don't follow you. She didn't disappear."

"No, Maureen didn't vanish in a cloud of smoke. That's true. But what if she distracted our attention long enough for the magician to blow the bank, then disappear?"

"It's a possibility," Tops agreed. "I worked with a woman once. Irene was a beauty, a desirable woman. She would sit at a table next to the card game. I would send a secret signal to her anytime I needed to get into the discards. She sneezed so loud that the buttons on her blouse popped off and her tits fell out. Every man at the table couldn't take his eyes off those pair of breasts. I had plenty of time to go through the discards. Now, that's a distraction."

"Only thing is, Maureen didn't vanish with the culprit."

"Maybe he's still around, waiting for her."

"Which makes me believe he's a townsman, a local working alone. Hell, Maureen is settled in for the night. No man in his right mind would wait for her. Not in this storm, he wouldn't. No, she didn't have anything to do with it. It was a coincidence she was here at the same time. The robber is probably in his shack, warming his hands over the stove, counting the cash. The guy knew his way around inside the bank. And in the dark." What Fargo didn't say was, if the robber knew where to find the strongbox, why didn't he know about the woodbin? Moreover, the robber was a tidy one. He'd taken the time to close the strongbox lid and replace the pried-apart lock.

Tops exposed his mentally alert mind when he suggested, "Yes, the bank robber is from Powderhorn.

Had to be. He knew storms like this one are common here in the evening at this time of year. He waited for one to occur at night. Thunder and lightning would mask the explosion."

"And blackpowder is handy to miners," Fargo added.

Miss Comely shouting that the bed was smoking hot ended their discussion. Fargo downed the remainder of his bourbon, then sauntered down the hall.

Roosters exchanging crows awakened him. Dawn had broken in clear skies. But they hadn't been clear long. Water dripped from the roof. Fargo reckoned he'd gotten all of twenty minutes sleep. He felt tired. Exhausted, in fact.

Fargo started peeling limbs off him, being careful to make no sudden movements lest he awaken them. Even in sleep the old whore's subconscious mind was alert, in tune with the presence of a man's body, ready to jolt her awake should that body stir. On the other hand Maureen seemed numb as he. He peeled Maureen first. A contortionist couldn't have extracted himself more skillfully than Fargo when getting out of Miss Comely's grasp. He crayfished straight down the bed and over the cold metal of the footboard. He quietly collected his shirt and other clothing, then stealthily made his way out of the room and into the saloon.

Tops lay curled up in a blanket on the floor in front of the fireplace. A mound of glowing embers warmed him. Fargo put another log on the fire and gently stoked the embers until a flame appeared. He sat to dress, then went outside and relieved himself in the muddy street. While doing it, he looked at the shadowy skeleton of Miss Comely's new Powderhorn saloon. He knew it couldn't possibly be completed before next spring; winter was just around the corner. A tragedy. He glanced to the bank.

He went behind the bank for a look-see in dawn's early light. The bank—what was left of it—stood in a quagmire. Quick would have to rebuild. He, too, was trapped in Powderhorn for the winter. Fargo walked through the debris looking for some kind of a clue to verify that the robbery had been committed by a miner. He found none.

Miss Comely's voice split the still, chilly morning air and set the roosters to crowing again. "Oh, yoo-hoo, Fargo, darling! I know you're around. I'm looking at your pretty horse. You wouldn't leave him for anything! Yoo-hoo! Come back, Fargo."

Chuckling, he began backing out the rear of the leaning structure. Something bright caught his eye. He paused and brought it into focus. A nail in the splintered framework encasing the vault door had snagged a tiny piece of white cloth. "I'm coming," he shouted to Miss Comely. Fargo stepped to the nail and removed the piece of cloth.

When he entered the saloon, he saw everyone awake and dressed. Tops was fixing breakfast over the coals in the hearth. The delicious aroma of bacon and eggs and stick biscuits and coffee flooded his nostrils. Miss Comely stood behind the bar, pouring herself a wake-up. Fargo moved to the lamp on the bar and held the cloth close to the light.

"What's that?" Miss Comely mumbled.

"A clue " Fargo answered. "Found it on a nail in the bank."

Maureen eased to the bar and looked at the piece of cloth.

In his peripheral vision, Fargo noticed her stiffen, then relax. He wondered if the artist had recognized the tiny piece of material, which he now saw had a splash of blue on it. He left it lying in the lamplight on the bar and stepped to a table and sat.

Maureen and Miss Comely joined him. Tops served

all three breakfast. Buttering a biscuit, Maureen opened the conversation. "Last night I heard you mention Tucson."

"That's correct. I'm heading that way right after I eat Tops' breakfast."

"Take me with you. I'll pay you a hundred dollars to get me there safely."

Fargo paused from sticking a piece of crisp fried bacon in his mouth. Going to Tucson with him clearly meant she had absolutely nothing to do with the bank being robbed. Without hesitation Fargo accepted the commission. "I agree to escort you on one condition."

Maureen smiled. Nodding, she said, "Anything. What is it?"

"I'm the boss. You do what I say, go where I lead."

"Agreed. Want payment now?" She reached for her hip pocket.

"No. When I get you there will be fine with me."

Again she nodded. "How long do you figure it will take to reach Tucson?"

"Depends," Fargo began, "on the weather between here and there. Three weeks at best, five or more if we get caught in high-country snow. And that's a possibility this time of year. I intend to ride a straight line to Tucson. Do you have cold-weather clothing?"

Maureen nodded.

"Why do you want to go to Tucson?" Miss Comely quizzed.

Maureen looked at her parfleche lying on the next table. "To sketch interesting scenes between here and there, then interesting faces, like Fargo's, after I get there. Why?" She glanced from Fargo to Miss Comely and back to him before explaining, "Art dealers in the East will pay a fortune for my work, scenes from the vanishing frontier." She shot Fargo a wink.

After that the breakfast was eaten in silence. Fargo downed a second cup of Tops' coffee, then pushed back from the table. "Are you ready for the trail?" He looked at Maureen.

"Yes. Soon as I pack the box and parfleche away." She stood.

Fargo shook hands with the men, embraced the two women. He handed Miss Comely his last five dollars, which she promptly handed back. "No, Fargo, my love, last night was worth every penny of it, and more. You made me feel young again." As she spoke, tears welled up in her eyes.

"The miners will come back," he muttered, "and the construction crew. Hang on till winter is over, then you'll see." He looked at Maureen and nodded toward the double doors.

Everyone stood on the porch to watch them mount up. Fargo touched the brim of his hat, then wheeled the Ovaro, nudged him to a walk, and rode out of Powderhorn.

Less than two miles out of town, Maureen angled off the trail and entered a grove of aspen.

Fargo halted. Turning in the saddle, he called to her, "Woman, where in hell are you going? You will get lost."

"No, I won't. I'm going to meet somebody."

3

Maureen Bodner disobeyed the Trailsman. He didn't like that. Watching her thread her horse through the stand of aspen, he shook his head in disgust. He grunted, then muttered under his breath, "Artists. I've never met one who isn't a mite crazy. This one takes the cake." Fargo called to her, "Dammit, woman, I'm ordering you to come back." She ignored him. He rode to the edge of the grove. She topped a knoll, then disappeared. Again he muttered under his breath, "Hardheaded female," then shouted into the aspen, "Twit, Tucson is this way."

This time Maureen answered. "I know. I told you I had to meet somebody."

He drew his Colt, made sure it was fully loaded, then followed her tracks over the knoll. At the bottom he saw she had turned left. And he got a whiff of smoke. It carried the aroma of coffee brewing. The "somebody" was fixing breakfast. Not knowing what he was riding into, but believing Maureen would not lead him into an ambush, he took the cautious approach, left her tracks, and rode parallel to them a short distance away. Shortly, he caught sight of her. He nudged the Ovaro into a lope to get ahead of her. Coming to an outcrop surrounded by thickets, he saw the smoke wafting lazily on the far side of them. Fargo halted, dismounted, and entered the outcrop. He drew his Colt, then parted the thickets.

Less than ten yards away stood a pack mule and a saddled dun mare exactly like the one Maureen rode. A bedroll lay open on the ground next to the cooking fire. The hunkered man had his back to Fargo. As the fellow reached for his coffeepot, Fargo thumbed back the Colt's hammer. Stepping through the thickets, he said, "Hold it right there, mister. Turn around slow and easy like."

The man rose with his hands up and twisted to face Fargo. Fargo's eyelids took to batting of their own accord. He shook his head in little quick jerks, for he couldn't believe what his eyes were seeing. He could hear Maureen's horse approaching off to the right and behind him, and he knew he had seen her astride the animal, therefore it wasn't possible the person staring at him was Maureen. He closed his eyes tightly, then opened one and looked at her anew.

"You going to shoot me, mister?"

Fargo could not believe what he heard: Maureen's voice. He glanced in the direction of the sound of her approaching horse, then asked, "How did you do it?"

"Do what?"

"Get out in front of me? Dismount and run?" Fargo didn't believe such a thing was possible, even though he suggested it. He eased the hammer down, holstered the Colt, and moved toward her. Coming closer, he saw he wasn't mistaken. She was Maureen, all right. Same face, same voice, same everything, right down to the clothes she wore.

"Who are you?" she queried. "Don't try any funny stuff," she warned.

"Funny stuff? What's it with you, anyhow? I've already been in your drawers more times than I care to remember. Funny stuff?" he repeated.

He was so focused on her that he didn't hear Maureen's horse walk up behind him until the animal halted and knickered. He glanced over his shoulder and did a double take. Maureen sat easy in the saddle. She smiled at him. Fargo backed up until both females were in his view.

The one astride the horse explained, "My mirror twin, Charleen. Charleen, meet our escort, Skye Fargo. He's the Trailsman." She eased out of the saddle.

"Escort?" snapped Charleen. "Sister, are you crazy?" Charleen shot a hateful look Fargo's way.

He trapped a groan.

Stepping to the coffeepot, Maureen said, "Fargo is going to escort us to Tucson. Aren't you, darling?" She squatted and filled a cup with the steaming brew.

"Tucson?" Charleen squalled. "I thought we—"

Maureen interrupted her. "I know, I know. Calm down, Sis, just calm down." Maureen handed Fargo the cup of coffee. Looking at him, she said, "We were going to Denver. But after last night I think it best we go to Tucson."

He noticed she had glanced at Charleen when she said "last night" and wondered what it meant. The identical twins obviously knew how to eye-talk. A quick glance said one thing, a lingering look another, a squint another, and so on. He would pay close attention to their eye-talking to determine what was left unspoken.

Charleen hissed, "Don't get any funny ideas about me, Mr. Fargo. I'm the exact opposite of my sister."

Maureen chuckled. "Don't let Sis's rotten attitude get under your skin, darling. Deep down she is a sweet person. A little clumsy at times, but nevertheless sweet as pumpkin pie."

Maureen did it again. Shot that same glance at her sister when she said "clumsy." They were eye-talking, all right.

Charleen said bitterly, "Sweet as pumpkin pie, my

ass. You're the one that's sweet . . . and clumsy. It gets you into trouble all the time."

Maureen laughed. Touching Fargo's hand, she cooed, "But I have all the fun. Isn't that right, darling?"

Fargo was ready for this line of thought to end. He didn't give a damn about Maureen's insatiable appetite for what she called fun, or Charleen's nasty attitude toward it. It looked as though he was stuck with both females. He hoped it would be a fast trip to Tucson. Fargo asked, "Charleen, are you an artist also?"

"Yes, I work in watercolors."

"Right- or left-handed," he wondered aloud. He recalled Maureen being right-handed when she sketched him, but ambidextrous as all hell, and lightning-fast, when in bed.

"Left," Charleen answered. "Why?"

"So I can tell you two apart. We are wasting daylight. Make up your minds about Tucson. I'll wait ten minutes for you to appear on the trail. After that I'm leaving." He turned and strode into the thicket.

Charleen muttered testily, "Well, of all the nerve. Sister, you really do know how to pick the sorriest of the lot."

Fargo chuckled, parted the limbs and went to his horse. Minutes later he heard the twins approaching on the far side of the knoll.

Charleen was lacing into Maureen, giving her holy hell for unilaterally changing their plans. "All you want is to get him between your legs."

"Uh, huh. As often as I can," Maureen replied.

Sight unseen, Fargo could tell them apart. While their voices were as identical as their appearances, Charleen always spoke hatefully, bitterly.

Charleen trailed the pack mule, a jenny. She appeared as sick and tired of Charleen's testy speech as Fargo, evidenced by the way she squinted and tried to lay her lopped ears back. Fargo saw an artist's easel tied to the top of the Jenny's burden. Two parfleches were under the easel. Maureen's wooden box hung from a large, bulging burlap bag on one side of the mule, a larger wooden box from the bag on the other side. He wondered what the bags held. The cooking and eating utensils rattled on twine secured behind the easel. He presumed the bags contained their food supplies.

Maureen moved up to ride alongside the Ovaro. Charleen hung back. Fargo heard her mumbling to herself. Maureen said, "Don't pay her any attention. She's just sulking. She will get over it. Wait and see."

Fargo didn't believe it. He nodded, anyhow.

They rode in near silence—only the plodding of hooves and the tinkling of utensils made any sounds— for about a mile, then Maureen spoke. "From time to time my sister or I will see an interesting scene worthy of capturing on paper. When we do, we will ask you to halt. Is that okay with you?"

"Fine by me. But I warn you not to tarry."

"Oh? Why?"

"Maureen, we have a long way to go before we reach the desert, and—"

"*Desert?*" she blurted. "What desert?"

"The one surrounding Tucson. I was about to say, I want to clear the Rockies, especially the high country, before the first snow flies. Otherwise, we will find ourselves trapped till the spring thaw."

"That would be fun."

"No, Maureen, it would not. Do you know what it is like to be caught in a blizzard for days on end—no, weeks or months—out in open country?"

"No," she admitted.

"It's a white hell. Colder than cold. Tree trunks snap like toothpicks. The ground and streams freeze solid. Game moves down into low country. That mule and our horses will starve to death unless they freeze to death first. Under those circumstances, people start killing and eating each other. Do you want to be with me under such a condition as that?"

Maureen shook her head, balefully. "I promise I'll not ask you to stop for scenes until we get to the desert," she said.

"Desert? What's this about a desert?" barked Charleen.

Maureen fixed a hard gaze onto her sister. Fargo thought he saw a message in it. Maureen said evenly, "Our mule is going to freeze to death."

The mule's ears tried to perk. The jenny launched into a seizure of loud hee-hawing that set the utensils to clattering. Charleen interrupted a belly laugh to say, "My God, Sister. *Freeze*? Freeze?" Charleen sliced the air with the heel of a hand to draw Maureen's attention. "Look around you. The trees are green. The birds sing. The creek gurgles. There's not one cloud in the sky. What makes you think it's going to freeze?" She cut her eyes at Fargo. "Did that big fool say that to upset you? Fill your head with scary talk? Huh, Sister, huh? Did he tell you it was going to turn cold?"

"I told her the truth," Fargo replied dryly. "I told her not to take too much time drawing pictures of interesting scenes. Storms like the one last night herald the first winter snow. While the sky is clear now, I promise you that storm clouds will burst over those mountains before the sun sets. The days will be sunny, the nights stormy. It will go on like that until the first snow flies. We better be on the desert when that happens. Cold rain you can suffer. Snow you cannot. I can survive both. So, what will it be, Charleen? Scenes or desert?"

"Desert," Maureen quickly answered.

Fargo looked at Charleen. Grim-jawed, she nodded.

"Then let's be on our way," Fargo muttered as he set the stallion to walking.

Three sunny days and three stormy nights later they rounded one of many bends in a deep, rock-walled canyon. The twins told him they needed to squat, that he should ride ahead and wait, that they would be along shortly. Fargo rode ahead.

He stood waiting beside on a big rock when he swore he heard Indians whooping. He cocked his head and listened more intently. The twins were back that way, somewhere between him and the sounds.

Within seconds he heard the unmistaken rumble that only fast-moving wagons make. He leaned away from the rock a tad and tried to see around the bend. Now he heard men shouting back and forth to one another, the crisp whack of reins being slapped on team's backs, hurrying them on, driving them faster and faster. The whooping and hollering grew louder, too. He also heard the twins start screaming.

Fargo was ready to run back to the twins when all hell came around the bend. The jenny led the procession. Her lop ears stood straight up. Her bulging eyeballs were as big as apples. She hee-hawed in panic. The utensils banged, the burlap bags flapped like wings on scared sparrows. The screaming twins charged at high speed in her dust.

No sooner had they cleared the bend than the first of six wagons skidded into view. Fargo closed his eyes tightly, shook his head in disbelief, then opened them and squinted through the jenny's dust. It was a woman gripping the reins all right, a woman with too much rouge on her cheeks. Bouncing around in the wagonbed behind her, trying their damnedest to grab hold of anything fixed, were six other females, all but one—she screamed the loudest—wearing too much rouge also. Fargo reckoned they were tarts.

Close behind the tart wagon came a wagon piled

high with kegs. The wide-eyed driver stood, balancing himself, slapping the reins on the lathered backs of the mule team. He shouted his fear to the team, "Begorra, damn you! Run for your dear life, Mazie. Else the redskins will feast on you."

The next wagon, also bulging with kegs and driven by a fear-stricken man skidded around the bend. Then came two other wagons filled with kegs. A fast-moving chuck wagon—Fargo thought it a modified Celerity—brought up the rear.

Then came the war-painted Indians, which Fargo recognized as being Ute. While they brandished toma-hawks, pogamoggans, scalping knives, bow and arrows, and carbines, not a shot had been fired by either the Ute or white men. Fargo frowned at that oddity.

The panic-stricken jenny and twins shot past Fargo in an all-out run. He withdrew his Sharps from its saddle case and prepared to start shooting any Indians who swerved toward the twins. But none did. The single-minded Ute focused on the wagons. Fargo mounted up and chased down the twins.

Maureen, unbridled fear on her face, screamed, "I don't want to die. Save me, Fargo! Save me from those savages."

He glanced at the savages, saw they had their backs to him.

"Save her, Mr. Fargo," screamed Charleen.

"From what?" Fargo asked in a calm voice.

"Shoot them," Maureen hollered. "Go shoot them. I'm scared."

"Stay here," Fargo told them. "Hide somewhere." He wheeled the Ovaro, set him into a dead run. The stallion reared, came down, and charged into the Indi-an's dust. His mane whipped, his shiny tail hiked and splayed. Fargo gave him free rein.

The pounding Ovaro caught up with the Ute warrior trailing the pack. The warrior looked over his shoulder at Fargo. The big man put a mean look on his face. The warrior smiled and moved over to let the pinto pass. The powerful black-and-white shot past the Indian pony.

So far not one shot had been fired.

Charging past the pack, Fargo and warriors exchanged glances. The warriors raised their weapons high, smiled, or cried a shrill war whoop. Fargo nodded to them.

The dust was so dense that Fargo nearly bumped into the rear end of the fast-moving chuck wagon. He swerved in time to prevent the crash. Coming abreast of the driver, Fargo shouted, "What in the hell is going on?"

The man's head snapped around. Fargo saw stark terror in the fellow's eyes. The driver yelled, "Fight 'em off, mister. Our teams are tiring. Fight 'em off."

Fargo pulled his Colt with one hand and the Sharps with the other. Pointing both weapons straight up, he commenced firing. Simultaneous with the first shot, he heard the warriors chorus a shriek, as though they were dumbfounded that he would shoot. The thundering pack halted immediately.

The driver raced on. He hollered, "Thanks, mister. Ride ahead. Stop the lead wagon."

Fargo glanced over his shoulder. The stunned, confused Ute milled about, looking at him. They weren't war-whooping. He dug his heels into the Ovaro's flanks. As he sped past the wagons, he shouted for each driver to slow down. "The redskins have given up the chase," he added.

Pulling alongside the lead wagon, Fargo shouted to the female driver, "Ma'am, you can whoa now. The Indians have left."

She tossed him a frightful glance, screamed, and slapped the reins on the team's backs.

Fargo yelled, "Dammit, lady, I said for you to stop."

She screamed again.

The big man moved the Ovaro up close alongside the lathered team, then leapt to land astride the lead horse. He whoaed the panting animal. Twisting around to face the woman, she blasted him with a barrage of French, not one word of it understood by him.

He looked past her at the other females who were rising from the wagonbed, peering wide-eyed at him. Six, including the driver, wore rouge on their cheeks, the seventh did not. All were shapely. All bombarded him in French.

Finally, the one barren of rouge shouted, "*Parlez-vous français*?"

That Fargo understood. He answered, "*Nein, fräulein*." It was the best he could do. He slid off the horse and stepped to the side of the wagon. He scanned their pretty faces and tight-fitting dresses. All but one, that is. She was grim-faced and dressed in black, wore no rouge. She snarled, "I don't belong here."

"Oh? And where do you belong?" Fargo wondered aloud, thoughtfully.

Before she could answer, two of the wagon drivers rushed up to Fargo. Broad grins spread on their sweaty faces as they shook his hands. One said, "Thanks, stranger, for saving us from those Injuns."

The other added, "Begorra, and a good thing you did."

Fargo gazed past them at the wagons and beyond. The Ute had disappeared, the dust settled. "Wait here," he muttered. "I'll be back."

They watched the big man mount up and ride back down the canyon. He found the twin's horses and the mule grazing on clumps of grass, the twins clutching each other, cowering behind a boulder. They shrieked when he said, "You two can come out now."

"Have you killed them?" gasped Maureen hopefully.

"All?" Charleen quickly added.

Fargo shook his head. "No, but I chased them away. We best go to the wagons. The Ute might come back."

"Come back?" Maureen peered over the boulder.

"Then it isn't over?" Charleen peered over the boulder.

"Come on," Fargo mumbled.

Approaching the wagons, Fargo saw everyone gathered next to the lead wagon. He rode to them, dismounted, and began asking questions. "Who are you people? Where are you going? The Ute are the friendliest people I know. Why were they attacking? What the hell's going on?" He pointed at a man wearing a green bowler, his eyelids blinking a mile a minute. "You give the answers."

The fellow stepped forward. His voice carried a thick Irish brogue when he said, "We're going to Miss Precious Goodbody's Golden Gully."

"Stop right there," Fargo ordered, blinking. "Miss Precious Goodbody's Golden Gully? You'd better explain that to me."

"Miss Precious' Gully is filled with gold."

Fargo blinked again. He refused to believe what he imagined. He mumbled, "I see. Go on."

"Miss Precious pissed on the gold."

"Er, uh, you better start over," Fargo said. "She pissed on the gold?" His brow furrowed.

Green Bowler pointed to a man. "Fools Gold O'Rourke, here, was with her."

Fools Gold broke a wide smile.

Fargo guessed the short, dumpy man's age at twenty-five. Fargo said, "Continue."

"Like I was saying, Fools Gold was with her and

saw the whole thing. They were the only ones in the gorge at the time. O'Rourke was prospecting. Miss Precious was with him for you know what."

"I get the picture," Fargo cut in. "Go on."

"Fools Gold panned and dug all over that gorge, but nary a flake nor nugget did he find. They moved to a gully Fools Gold had already worked. Miss Precious went up one side of it and took a piss. Just like cats do, she looked at where she had leaked. The tip of a vein of gold gleamed in the dew.

"O'Rourke came and took a look, then started digging around the find. The vein went straight into that side of the gully. The more he dug, the bigger the vein got. Fools Gold covered it up with dirt. He told Miss Precious to sit on it and not move, that he was going to Denver to get us to help work Miss Precious Goodbody's Golden Gully. We came and started digging in her hole."

"I bet you did," Fargo replied wryly. "Is she still around?"

Green Bowler nodded. "Oh, yeah. She's with the rest of the boys at the mine."

"Well, that explains that," Fargo began. He nodded toward the tarts. "Now, them. By the way, what's your name?"

"Blinky O'Brien," Blinky answered, blinking. An evil grin formed on his lips when he continued, "Miss Precious needed some relief, what with so many of us needing her. We stole the Frenchies back in Denver."

Fargo looked at the one wearing no rouge. Following his gaze, Blinky explained rather sheepishly, "She was a mistake. A big mistake. We're sorry we took her, too. Didn't realize it till she woke up. By that time we were well on our way back to the gorge. We couldn't leave her stranded and we didn't want to take her any farther. A high-toned woman she is. But she does talk French."

"What's your name, ma'am?" Fargo asked even though he was sure of her answer.

"Grace Hatfield," she drawled, bittersweet syrupy. "I'm ordering you to return me to Denver. I don't belong with these, these . . . fallen women, God save their souls."

Fargo ignored her. He asked Blinky, "Why did the Ute attack and not fire a shot?"

Blinky nodded toward the other wagons. "They didn't shoot because they were afraid they'd miss and blow a hole in one of the kegs. That's why."

"What's in the kegs, anyhow?" Fargo queried. "I see four wagons piled high with them."

"Good Irish whiskey," Blinky said. "Barely enough to last through the winter. We can't afford to lose one drop."

And that explained that, Fargo told himself.

Before he could ask the next question, Blinky answered it. "Each year Chief Crossed-Eyes lays in wait for us in this here canyon. Each year his braves attack screaming and whooping and try to steal our whiskey. So far we've been lucky. But this time Crossed-Eyes nearly caught us. Mister, we'll pay you and your guns a thousand dollars in gold to get us back to the gorge safe and sound."

Charleen replied, "Mr. Fargo accepts."

Fargo cut his eyes to her. "I thought you two were all fired up to get to Tucson?"

Maureen muttered lamely, "Fargo, darling, there's safety in numbers. Please help these poor men and ladies."

Fargo scratched his beard. "How far is it to the gorge, Blinky?"

"Not far. Six days at the most."

The Trailsman didn't like that length of time. He looked at the dark thunderheads building in the west. "On one condition," he said.

"Anything," Blinky said. "Ask and you have my word on it."

"You people do what I say."

All the Irishmen nodded.

Fargo said, "Leave a keg on the trail where the Ute can find it."

The Irishmen took on pained expressions, became restless, groaned a lot. Grimacing, Blinky pulled his green bowler down until his ears flopped. He whined, "Please, oh, please, mister—you don't know what you're asking. That whiskey is our life blood."

"One keg," Fargo repeated.

Reluctantly they obeyed. Fargo watched the Irishmen remove a keg from the next wagon in the line and stand it on the ground. They looked at him most pitifully, as though losing a dear, dear friend, and started shedding tears.

Fargo told them to get in their drivers' seats and head out.

In the west, lightning flashed, thunder boomed. Fargo wanted to clear the canyon before the storm struck. He set a quick pace.

4

Fargo rode alongside the lead wagon so he could chat with the driver, Trevor O'Malley. The twins rode between Trevor's and the tart's wagon. Every now and then Fargo checked the western horizon to see how close the black clouds were getting and to estimate when they would boil into the canyon. The storm clouds looked unusually ugly. Fargo knew he and the others were in for a hell of a night. His problem was what to do with the French tarts, Grace Hatfield, and the twins. They would be hard-put-out in the open during the storm. The men could look out for themselves. They were accustomed to the hard life.

Fargo asked Trevor, "How much longer are we going to be in this canyon?"

"Not much. About two more hours. Horror Canyon opens to a wide but short valley we call Meditation Valley."

"Horror Canyon?"

"Uh, huh. Horrible things, such as those crazy Ute, always happen in Horror Canyon. The next one is worse."

O'Malley thought horrible things lurked in Horror Canyon. Obviously he considered a few friendly Ute in need of drink as being horrible. Fargo did not. He asked about the worse one.

"Worser Canyon? It twists and turns more than a sidewinder. Them shear rocky walls go way up. Barely enough room on the trail for the wagons. Rocks are always falling. Big rocks. Big enough to flatten a wagon. We gotta get this whiskey—*all* of it—to the Shamrock safe and sound."

"Shamrock?"

"Uh, huh. That's the name of our place in the gorge. We built it with our own hands so's Miss Precious could have a place to sprawl in."

Fargo had visions of a rickety structure. He'd seen plenty at the mining sites he visited. Miners lived much like moles. Nodding toward the rear, Fargo asked, "What the tart's names?"

"Don't rightly know, not talking their language and all. Feisty lot, they are. But we gave them names. We call the one driving Can Can. She's their madam. Fancy that. We got ourselves a real madam. The others were named Mimi, Déjà Vu, Oui Oui, and Ooolala. The boys at the Shamrock are gonna be happy when they see we brought back tarts."

"How did Grace Hatfield get mixed in with them?"

"We don't screw that woman," O'Malley grunted. "Anybody goes near that woman, she starts quoting the holy Bible. King James' version. Knows it by heart, she does. In one of her sane periods she said she was from Pascagoula, Mississippi, crusading for the Lord, sweet Jesus, on the frontier. Claims God told her to go and do it. Claims God spoke to her from a burning mulberry bush.

"Anyhow, Grace was with the tarts when we stole them. She had her Bible open, giving them hellfire and brimstone in their own language. We thought she was one of them, so we took her right along with the others. Blinky O'Brien had gotten a hold of a bottle of ether. We soaked rags in it and clamped the rags over the tart's mouths and noses. Went right to sleep, they did. Then we put their limp bodies in a wagon Barney O'Neal stole."

"What happened to Barney?" Fargo quizzed.

"I'm getting to that part. We kept knocking them tarts out with the ether till we were good and far out of Denver. When that woman woke up and saw O'Neal sitting there in the driver's seat, she started in on him, giving Barney holy hell. I mean to tell you that woman yelled and hollered at Barney so loud that us other drivers had to drop back about a mile to keep from hearing her ravings.

"O'Neal put up with her as long as he could. Next thing we knowed Barney came running to us. Barney, he was insane out of his mind. He had that same look in his eyes what crazy folks have. Spit run out of the corners of his mouth. Barney has red hair, same as me. Well, in the short time that woman had Barney cornered, screeching at him, she scared him so much that a two-inch-wide pure-white streak showed up in his hair. We grabbed him and tried to calm him down. Barney, he was shaking to pieces. He told us nothing was worth putting up with that woman. Barney told us we could have his part of the gold. Then he took off running back down the trail, heading for Denver. That's the last we saw of Barney O'Neal." O'Malley shook his head sorrowfully.

Fargo changed the subject. "How much gold do you Irishmen have? What are your plans for it?"

"Plans? Don't rightly know. We've been so busy working the mine that we haven't laid any plans. We got a lot of gold. It's piled up in a shed we built. The mine shaft goes way down inside the gully. Mister, there isn't no end to that vein of gold. The deeper we dig, the bigger it gets. Maybe we'll buy Denver when it plays out."

"Have you sold any of it?"

"Not an ounce. We're not fools, you know. Claim-jumpers would pour into the gorge if it was knowed we struck it rich. We don't tell anybody when we go to Denver for the winter whiskey."

Fargo frowned. "So, where do you get the money to buy the whiskey?"

"From Miss Precious. She's rich."

"Uh, you mean she had money before she pissed on the gold?"

"Lots of it. So much a pack mule had to carry it."

Fargo looked behind at the jenny. He wondered aloud, "Where do you reckon Miss Precious got it?"

"Beats hell out of me. I've never asked, and she hasn't said. All I know is she had it when she got with Fools Gold O'Rourke back in Denver."

"When was that, O'Malley? What were the circumstances?"

"Three years ago. Fools Gold said Miss Precious and the pack mule staggered out of the smoke and bumped into him. She told him to take her as far away from Denver as fast as he could. He was going prospecting at the time, so he took her with him."

"Staggered out of smoke?" Fargo queried.

"Fools Gold told us nigh on a whole block in Denver blowed up and caught fire. Miss Precious and the mule came out of the smoke. Anyhow, she pays for the whiskey and supplies."

Fargo had heard enough. Glancing at the darkening sky, he decided he would ride ahead and scout for a cave or shelter of some kind. He told O'Malley what he was going to do, then set the pinto into a lope and headed down Horror Canyon. After riding about two miles and not spotting shelter, he turned back. A cool, moisture-laden breeze chased him. He heard thunder.

Coming alongside O'Malley's wagon, Fargo suggested, "Let's see if we can beat this storm. I don't want to be in this canyon when it strikes. Set a fast pace, Trevor. I'll tell the others."

O'Malley popped his reins on the team's backs.

Fargo rode to the rear, urged everyone to quicken their pace, then moved up and joined the twins.

Maureen sighed and smiled, Charleen cut hateful eyes at him. "Ma'am, is something stuck in your craw?"

Charleen hissed, "You nearly got us killed. We're paying you good money to get us to Tucson in one piece. You—"

"Whoa, young lady," Fargo broke in. "You two want to head straight for Tucson, it's fine with me. I'll tell O'Malley and the others the deal is off with them." Fargo nudged the Ovaro.

Maureen stopped him. "No, no, Skye, darling. Don't do that." She glanced at Charleen. "Apologize, Sis."

"Hunh," Charleen snorted. Then she changed the subject but not her nasty tone of voice. "I know your kind, Mr. Fargo. Big, muscled man like you. You think all you need to do is snap your fingers for women to lay down and spread their legs. You make me sick. You're after those whores. Can't wait to get your hands on them."

"No, he's not," Maureen censured. "Skye wouldn't think of doing such a thing. Isn't that right, Skye, darling?"

Riding up to the lead wagon, he shook his head.

The storm clouds blotted out the sunset. Darkness fell on Horror Canyon. The wind picked up. Lightning split the roiling clouds, stabbed down, and peeled a Douglas fir atop the wall on Fargo's left. Thunder boomed and rumbled in the canyon. A light rainfall preceded a torrential downpour.

O'Malley hollered, "Meditation Valley is just around the next bend!" He beat the reins on the team's backs.

Lightning flashed and Fargo saw the bend. More lightning flashed. He saw the canyon narrowed considerably at the bend. He dropped back to see how the others were doing. All were encouraging their teams to move faster.

In the darkness and heavy rain, it was next to impossible for Fargo to see. Through the thunder and cracks of lightning he heard O'Malley scream, "Aw, shit. Whoa! Goddammit, I said whoa."

He rode ahead as the wagons lurched to a halt. Lightning flashed. He saw O'Malley hunkered behind the driver's seat, peering over its backrest. And Fargo saw why he had stopped. Rocks littered the narrow bend. Passage was impossible.

As Fargo stared at the blockage, six big bolts of lightning struck the rocks. They sizzled and they exploded in the blinding flashes. A mammoth boom of thunder shook the muddy ground. Then another, and another. The women were screaming. The Irishmen were screaming. Fargo twisted in his saddle to tell them to shut up. Before he could, a massive bolt of lightning blasted down, struck behind the rocky barrier, exploded, and lit up Horror Canyon. He spun around in time to see the bolt's blue-white, garish brilliance . . . and a man standing with his feet apart on top of the rocks.

The man brandished a pair of flintlock pistols. His hat was triangular, his blouse loose-fitting, his trousers baggy, and he wore knee-high boots the likes of which Fargo had never seen. The man shouted through his unruly blue-black beard, "Yo, ho, me buckos. It's a prize vessel Blue-blackbeard sees. Off with their heads, boys."

As he spoke eight other similarly dressed men rose from behind the rocks. Fargo drew his Colt. O'Malley's team of mules took to bucking, kicking, hee-hawing, and that set the other teams to acting up. O'Malley's mules bumped into the Ovaro. Fargo held his fire, waited for one of the men to shoot first. None did.

Instead, they rushed forward, by-passed O'Malley's wagon altogether. Two started pulling the twins off their mounts. Others began yanking tarts from the tart wagon. Fargo managed to back the stallion from between O'Malley's wagon and the rocky wall of the bend. He jumped to the muddy ground and commenced pistol-whipping the snarling, growling men. He wrestled the screaming twins free from two men's grasps, knocked the men's heads together. Then he ran to the tart wagon.

Men had the screaming tarts draped over their shoulders. Their leader's voice roared through the hellish booming of thunder, "Avast, me laddies! Take the treasure back to the Skull and Crossbones."

Fargo saw Grace Hatfield draped over the leader's shoulder. Rushing to rescue her, he collided with another tart-carrying man. Fargo paused to rescue her. He sent the scoundrel fleeing with a knot on his noggin. Then he saved another tart. Then another, till he reckoned he had rescued them all. The men vanished as quickly as they had appeared. Only the hard wind, rain, lightning, and thunder remained.

Fargo took a headcount. Everyone was accounted for, except Grace Hatfield. O'Malley said, "Good riddance."

Fools Gold echoed O'Malley's sentiment.

But testy Charleen snarled, "Mr. Fargo, I order you to go save that poor woman."

He intended to do just that, anyhow. He told the Irishmen, "Start clearing the trail. They were on foot. Shouldn't be hard to find. I'll be back shortly."

They watched him mount up. He squeezed past O'Malley's wagon, then dug his heels into the Ovaro's flanks. The rock barricade presented no problem for the powerful stallion. He cleared it with room to

52

spare, hit the ground running. With nowhere else to go—the sheer canyon walls prevented all other avenues of escape—Fargo knew the culprits fled to Meditation Valley. In the valley he rode a switchback course to make sure he didn't pass the skunks in the night. And well he did, for upon completing the third leg he heard Grace yell, "Leave me alone, you brutes. The wages of sin is death. Oh, my God, puleeze stop. That hurts." The men laughed.

Fargo was on them before they realized it. The leader had his pants down, lying between Grace's legs, held apart by two of the others, plunging into her at a fast rate. Fargo drew his Sharps, dismounted, and started swinging the barrel at them. The men yelped, scattered, and ran. The one he wanted, though, made a fight of the untimely interruption in his fun.

Rising, he pulled his pants up and growled, "I'll have your head, bucko, for doing this. Nobody—jackleg seaman or the king's best—makes a fool out of Blue-blackbeard and gets away with his head. Pistols, knives, or fists?"

Fargo slid the Sharps into its saddle case, fell into a crouch, and began circling Blue-blackbeard. Blue-blackbeard parried, chuckling. Naked Grace knelt in the center of the circling men. Hands over her bosom, Grace sobbed, "You ruined me, you bastard."

Fargo worked his way close to Blue-blackbeard, tempted him with a clumsy move that created an opening. Blue-blackbeard took the invite. He lunged and tackled Fargo around the waist. Fargo pounded on Blue-blackbeard's kidneys. Groaning painfully, the fellow let go and grabbed Fargo's throat. Clasping his hands, the big man brought them up fast between his adversary's arms and pushed outward as he did. The sudden movement knocked Blue-blackbeard away. The man was wide open for an uppercut. Fargo threw one. It slammed against Blue-blackbeard's jaw. Fargo heard bone crack as the man catapulted backward, unconscious before he splattered the mud.

Grace stood, protected her crotch and bosom, while staring wide-eyed at the victor. When Fargo came to her, fully intending to take her arm and help her get into his saddle, she screamed and pounded her fists on his chest. "God, save me," Grace hollered heavenward. Lightning and thunder answered.

So did the Trailsman. "Lady, God sent me to save your ass." He grabbed Grace around the waist and put her in the saddle. Shoving her against the saddlehorn, he eased up behind her.

She cried, "Owee! You beast, your pommel is raping me." She squirmed the crack of her buttocks into Fargo's crotch.

He set the Ovaro to walk and rode out of Meditation Valley to the bend and wagons. He saw the Irishmen had moved the rocks to one side of the trail to allow just enough room for the wagons to get through. O'Malley and Fools Gold were rolling the last rock out of the way.

Fools Gold groaned, "Aw, shit, you found her."

Fargo was soaked to the skin, tired from fighting, and his belly growled to be fed. He wasn't in the mood to put up with Fools Gold's shit, nor any of the others. He growled, "Head 'em up and move 'em out. Get in those driver's seats and start rolling." When they just stood there openmouthed, Fargo roared, "Now!"

The Irishmen fled to their seats.

Fargo led the wagons into Meditation Valley. He halted next to an outcrop on high ground, dismounted, and stood Grace on the ground. He asked Wee Willie if he had a sheet of canvas in the chuck wagon. Wee Willie nodded. Fargo told him to get it.

Gotcheye O'Toole and Blinky O'Brien helped Fargo spread and tie down the canvas over a wide space in the outcrop. Then he told everyone to get in out of the rain.

Charleen balked. "Mr. Fargo, there's too many of us to get under that flimsy shelter. I want the men to stay outside. They would take liberties on us ladies. I don't want their filthy hands touching me."

Maureen mumbled, "I don't mind."

Fools Gold whined, "Not another one."

Fargo ordered, "Everyone under the canvas. Charleen, you can do what you like."

Charleen was the first to get under the canvas shelter.

Wee Willie fetched beef jerky from the chuck wagon and passed it around. Munching on a piece of jerky, Fargo asked O'Malley, "All right, now that it is over, who were those bastards? Their leader called himself Blue-blackbeard."

"He's a pirate," O'Malley answered evenly.

Fargo couldn't believe his ears. "Pirate? An honest-to-God swashbuckling pirate?"

"Yep. That he is . . . or was. Blue-blackbeard gave up plundering on the high seas. Him and his crew now work the Skull and Crossbones mine. Got a pirate flag and everything."

"You know them?" Fargo was a mite dumbfounded.

"Of course. They pounce on us every year at the bend."

Fargo shook his head to clear it of the fuzzies.

O'Malley continued, "They were after our whiskey. But I guess they smelled the tarts. Plenty of good company during the long winter nights all snowed in is ten times better than getting drunk."

"Where is the Skull and Crossbones?"

" 'Bout a three-day hike from the bend. Blue-blackbeard don't have any horses or mules. He and his men walk to the Shamrock twice a year to lay Miss Precious. She don't mind. She claims it's a welcome change. Anyhow, they always walk away with satisfied looks on their mugs."

First the Utes, then pirates-turned-miners. Fargo wondered what next? He asked, "Tell me again how far to the gorge."

"Six days from Meditation Valley."

"And we have to pass through Worser Canyon?"

"Uh, huh. Then Mean Canyon. On the far end of Mean is Big Windy. Then comes Trouble Canyon. It and Deadly Canyon are separated by Snake Valley. Deadly is the last canyon. It empties into Blood Gorge, home."

"Blood Gorge?"

"Uh, huh. That's because all the rocks there are flecked blood-red."

Fargo looked at Grace. "Are you all right, ma'am?"

"I'm fine, no thanks to your hard pommel and your harder nudging in my rear end."

"Fargo, you didn't?" gasped Maureen.

"Sure he did," Charleen answered. "He's a sick man."

Fargo ignored her caustic remarks. He leaned his back to the outcrop, pulled his hat down over his eyes, relaxed, and drifted into sleep, wondering if he could clear the Rockies before it snowed. He regretted bumping into the Irishmen.

After midnight the wind suddenly ceased blowing. Rain stopped falling. The thunder rumbled away, into Horror Canyon. The lightning flickered out. Only the dark clouds remained. All was quiet.

Until that woman screamed.

5

Grace hollered, "Leave me alone! Genesis nineteen, twenty-six. Stop it."

Fargo heard flesh slap flesh, then a grunt. Mumbling a stretch of scripture, Grace crawled by him. She stood and braced herself on the edge of the outcrop.

Fargo said, "Put some clothes on. You'll catch a cold in this weather."

"I don't have any," she replied bitterly. "The bastards ripped and tore my dress—everything—from my body. Bastards!"

Well, Fargo thought, the high-tone woman lost her maidenhead and learned how to cuss in exchange. Remarkable. He suggested, "Ask Oui Oui and the other ladies if they can loan you some clothes. At least a pair of bloomers."

"They don't have any extra clothing. These Godless Irishmen—papists all—said we wouldn't need any where we were going. God, I'm cold. I've got goosebumps all over me. Damn!"

Grace was getting dirty-mouthed. He peered under the canvas. "Any you men got spare clothes Miss Hatfield can borrow?"

"No," Blinky O'Brien answered.

Gotcheye O'Toole added, "We got on all we have."

Wee Willie O'Hoolihan explained, "These are our city clothes."

Fools Gold O'Rourke explained Wee Willie's explanation. "We go naked in the gorge."

O'Malley explained Fools Gold's explanation. "We stay ready for Miss Precious."

Fargo asked, "You twins have spare clothes?"

"Let her freeze, for all I care," Charleen hissed. "The shameless hussy got what she deserved."

"No, I didn't," Grace retaliated.

"Oh, yes you did," Charleen persisted. "I saw you wink at that pirate."

"No, I didn't," Grace repeated. "A drop of rain got in my eyes. It caused me to blink."

Maureen said, "I will let you have a pair of pants and a shirt."

"No, you won't," Charleen spat. "She's too fat for our pants. She'd split them wide open."

"I'll go naked," Grace replied. "I'd die before wearing your precious clothes."

Fargo was ready for their bickering to come to a halt. He whistled to the Ovaro. The stallion trotted up to him with ears perked. Fargo dug his duster out of his bedding and handed it to Grace. "Here. Wear this." Then he scooted back inside the outcrop. "I don't want to hear another word out of any of you. Got that, boys? As for me, I'm going to get some badly needed shut-eye." Fargo rolled onto his side and went to sleep.

The aromas of coffee brewing and bacon frying awakened the big man. He sat to stretch and yawn. Dawn's early light had broken. All signs of last night's storm had disappeared. The sky was clear. An owl hooted. The air was still. Everyone had gathered at Wee Willie's chuck wagon for breakfast. Fargo studied them. A motley bunch of matched misfits, he decided. The tarts spoke in low tones. They looked tired, as though sleep had passed them by. The Irishmen appeared even more tired—exhausted, in fact. Whereas the tarts either stood with their arms folded at their bosoms or leaned against the side of the chuck wagon, the Irishmen sprawled on the cool, wet grass. The twins and Grace sat close to Wee Willie's cooking fire, watching him prepare the meal. Nobody held a tin cup.

Fargo crawled out from under the canvas. All eyes cut toward him. He saw a mixture of unmitigated fear and awe in their expressions. The fear and awe, he reckoned, were caused by the same thing—his no-nonsense attitude. At the same time they wanted to be told what to do and to have their own way, and left him to choose between the two. During an attack, they were willing, even eager, to obey his orders. After the attack, they wanted to revert to habit, as though it never happened. "So soon they forget," he mumbled under his breath. Fargo stood and stretched again.

He went to the Ovaro and got his tin cup. At the fire he held it out for Wee Willie to fill. "The bacon smells good," Fargo complimented.

Wee Willie smiled. "Wait till you smell my biscuits."

Taking a sip of the steaming brew, Fargo looked over the rim of the cup at Grace. She sat staring into the fire. Grace Hatfield's nocturnal experience with the big pirate had obviously caught up with her. What was she thinking about it, Fargo wondered, and finally asked.

Grace didn't take her blank gaze off the flames when she answered hollow-voiced, as though resigned to the reality, "I'm sore as hell, no thanks to you. That son of a bitch wallowed me good. I can still feel him stretching me down there. Shit, I'll never be the same again." She looked at Fargo and added, "I'm a fallen woman, same as these tarts."

Fargo nodded. He shifted his gaze to Charleen.

"You look like you want to say something to me. Spit it out. Clear the air for all to hear."

Glowering, Charleen rose. She snarled, "You're a vile, contemptible man, Mr. Fargo. You let those pirates capture Grace on purpose. You knew she was a virgin, pure as the driven snow."

No, he didn't know that, he told himself, but said, "Go on." He wanted to hear the purpose.

"I saw Blue-blackbeard carrying Grace away. So did you. You let him take her, knowing full well what he would do to her. And he did. I'd be willing to wager you hoped all of us would be carried away and violated by those pirates, too. You men are all alike. If you can't get at an innocent female yourself—if you're not man enough to respect her purity until marriage— you stand by and let another filthy man do the job, *then* you come to her and cover her naked body with a duster. I know what you're up to, Mr. Fargo."

"Er, what, exactly?" Fargo queried. He glanced at Grace.

Charleen continued, "You're thinking now that she's not pure, there is no reason for Grace to deny your advances on her. Contemptible thinking, Mr. Fargo. Vile, nasty and contemptible. I despise you."

Fargo looked at Grace and told her to tell the Frenchwomen what Charleen said.

She spoke to Charleen instead. "You are wrong about Mr. Fargo. He did not stand and allow Blue-blackbeard to carry me off. My God, Charleen, those men stormed in. There were so many of them that it is amazing he saved as many of you as he did. Thanks to no help from these cowardly Irishmen. All they were interested in saving was their precious whiskey. I saw Mr. Fargo save your sorry ass, and your sister's, too. You, Charleen Bodner, are the one who is contemptible. You gladly sacrificed my ass to save your own." Then she translated to the tarts.

Fargo watched the tarts eyes dart from him to Charleen as Grace spoke. When Grace fell silent, all of the tarts smiled at Fargo.

Charleen snorted, "This is disgusting."

They watched her walk out into the meadow a ways and stop.

Wee Willie brought pans of biscuits out of a stove oven tied to the back of the chuck wagon. He aimed his spatula at Charleen, but spoke to Fargo. "She's in a huff. All swole up bigger'n a Texas horny toad. Looks just as mean as one, too."

Fargo took two biscuits. Buttering them, he said, "Here, Maureen, take these biscuits to your twin. Tell her to quit sulking, that we have a long way to go. My patience wears mighty thin when around angry females on a long trip."

"Charleen doesn't mean it, Skye. Sis will be all right. Wait and see." Maureen took the biscuits and headed toward Charleen.

Fargo carried his tin plate of food and cup of coffee to the outcrop. He ate four biscuits, three fried eggs, and some bacon, then washed all of it down with coffee. As he ate and drank, he studied the Irishmen. Not a bad lot, he decided. Hardworking, fun-loving men. Whiskey-drinkers all. They were quick to smile. Fargo liked that. And they had humor. Anybody who can name canyons Horror and Worser has to have the capacity to look the devil in the eye and laugh at him. He wondered if Miss Precious would prove to be anything like they projected her to him.

His gaze wandered to Grace Hatfield, sitting next to the fire, munching absent-mindedly on a biscuit. He wondered what she was thinking.

A movement by the twins drew his attention to them. They were walking toward the chuck wagon, their arms around each other's waist. They too were a study in contradictions, albeit different from Grace.

Here the mirror effect came into play. While the reflected image was the same, the personalities were the exact opposite. Or were they? Maybe they are one, he mused. Split into two look-alike bodies. In the final analysis, he decided, what Maureen's personality says and does, Charleen's is probably in full agreement, and vice-versa. Maureen, the playful, free-spirited of the two; Charleen, the conscience that forever tried to control that free spirit and hide it . . . and failed. Fargo concluded Maureen and Charleen possessed the same personality. Neither of the external two dominated. Maureen mirrored Charleen's passions. What he found with Maureen, he would also find with Charleen. Because their personalities were really one, it was impossible to separate them.

Watching them stroll arm-in-arm toward the chuck wagon, Fargo couldn't tell which was which. He untied and folded the sheet of canvas and carried it and his empty cup and plate to the wagon. Glancing at the brightening sky, he said, "I'm ready for Worser Canyon. You scallawags get in the wagons. Let's see if we can get this good Irish whiskey to Blood Gorge without spilling another drop."

That was music to the Irishmen's ears. Smiles blossomed on their faces. They hurried to help Wee Willie store his stuff, then hurried even faster to their wagons.

Fargo rode out of Meditation Valley to scout Worser Canyon. He halted in the opening and scanned the tops of the walls. While he didn't see anything amiss, the hairs on his nape tingled, a sure signal that something was indeed not as it should be. He rode deeper into the canyon, constantly keeping his eyes on the jagged tops of the ridges, watching for signs. After riding about a quarter-mile and spotting no signs of impending danger, he reined the stallion to a halt and twisted in the saddle to see if the wagons were coming.

Wee Willie's chuck wagon had taken the lead position. The chuck wagon was just entering the canyon. Fargo sat easy in the saddle while he waited for Wee Willie to catch up to him. The Trailsman's keen vision missed nothing as he studied what lay ahead. A river, long since redirected, had carved away loose soil and left deep, rocky overhangs on both sides of the canyon. On top of the overhanging ledges, trees grew: blue spruce, pine, and in sunny places, aspen. The ledges weren't too wide. At the back of them, sheer rocky walls rose. And on top of their sawtooth ridges, the trees began again. The floor of the canyon lay flat and smooth, interrupted in places by remains of minor landslides. Less than a half-mile away, a sharp bend prevented him from seeing any farther. But Fargo presumed around the bend was more of the same terrain. He saw nothing that didn't belong.

The chuck wagon rumbled past Fargo. He nudged the Ovaro to follow alongside Wee Willie. The Irishmen asked, "Having yourself a look-see?"

Fargo nodded.

Wee Willie trapped a chuckle. "This is the pretty part. It gets worser around that bend yonder. When the wind blows just right, it sounds like a witch wailing. Nearly scares the pants off me. I can't get out of Worser Canyon fast enough."

"Why do you follow this route, anyway, Wee Willie? Best I recollect there are several trails in these parts better than the one we are on."

"That's true," Wee Willie agreed. "Only thing is, they're too narrow in places for the wagons. Those trails go up and down and around. Fine for a man on a horse, but mighty treacherous for wagons with teams. We found this series of canyons is faster, safer."

"Safer?" Fargo cut his eyes to Wee Willie and chuckled.

The Irishman blushed. He realized he had made a *faux pas*. Lamely, he tried to correct it. "You mean the Utes and pirates?"

"Damn right. I never saw such a thing. If the twins and I had not stopped, you guys would have missed us. What in the world are you doing unarmed in raw, open country? Have you lost your senses? Between Chief Crossed-Eyes and his warriors, and Blue-blackbeard and his pirate rogues, they could have stripped your wagons clean as a hound's tooth without firing a shot. And, I might add, taken the tarts, left you blinking open-mouthed at one another. You call that safe?"

"Well, er, uh, we woulda thunk of something. We always do."

"Like what, pray tell?"

Fargo watched Wee Willie's eyes roll back, obviously in thought. The best Wee Willie could come up with in the way of an answer was an indecipherable mumble. "Such as that," he finally said clear as a bell.

Shaking his head, Fargo grimaced.

Wee Willie changed the subject. "How do you tell those twins apart? We can't."

"Just looking at them, I can't tell them apart. The difference comes in their voices, and then only in the manner in which they speak. Charleen is the bitchy one. Other than that, there is no difference. I should say no apparent difference." He noticed a puzzled expression form on the Irishman's face. "It's complicated, Wee Willie. You have to understand contradictions."

Wee Willie squinted and frowned, stared at his reins. Finally he said, "I see what you mean."

Fargo doubted he did. Fargo doubted "complicated" and "contradiction" were in Wee Willie's vocabulary. A simple man, Wee Willie, like the other men, lived an unencumbered life, void of complications and contradictions. In that respect they were childlike. If they had ever known the harsh realities of the real world, and Fargo assumed they had, Blood Gorge provided their escape from these realities. He imagined their day consumed by the simple life: digging, drinking, lying with Miss Precious. What more could a man-child ask for? Fargo wondered. What more did he need? Far be it for him to tinker with a good thing. Fargo dropped back to the tart wagon.

The tarts, and Grace Hatfield, too, flashed big smiles at him. He touched the brim of his hat. " 'Morning, ladies."

Grace translated to the tarts. They chorused, "*Bon jour, grand homme.*"

"Where did you learn how to speak French?" Fargo inquired. "What did they say?"

"We were poor folk, Mr. Fargo. Dirt poor. They said, 'Good morning, big man.' "

He didn't see how that had anything to do with her learning how to speak French. Poor, rich, had nothing to do with it. Besides, poor, dirt poor, was relative. "Compared to what?" he mused aloud. "In some ways these Irishmen are poor as hell; in others, rich as country butter."

"Penniless poor, Mr. Fargo. All we had was the holy Bible to see us through that hell and misery back in Pascagoula. King James' version." Grace reached under the driver's seat. She retrieved and opened her Bible.

Fargo just knew Grace was going to preach at him. He didn't want to hear it. Not this morning.

Grace apparently saw him nudge the stallion's flanks. She blurted. "Don't you want to hear how I learned French?"

He checked the nudge. "Er, what's that Bible got to do with it?"

"Everything . . . and nothing."

Neither was Fargo in any mood for riddles. He squinted at Grace, clearly implying she should get on with it.

She said, "Auggie Harlow and I were the same age. Ten. We'd sit in the shade of a big elm growing on the bank of the creek and read this Bible while dangling our feet in the water. Auggie's family didn't have a Bible. Not that it mattered because none of the Harlows could read or write. I used the Bible to teach Auggie how to read. And I learned scriptures forward and backward in the process. Memorized them, in fact.

"One spring day six years later Auggie said she would meet me under our elm. She never came. Not that day, not ever again. I went looking for her at the Harlows' place. Her little brothers told me Auggie had run off. Naturally I was concerned, so I asked where to. They said to Pascagoula."

"How did you learn French?" Fargo persisted.

"I'm coming to that. So I walked to Pascagoula. After asking around, a big strapping lad told me a new girl from the swamps had started working in Miss St. Claire's bordello. I informed him in no uncertain terms that that swamp girl wasn't my Auggie."

"But she was," Fargo cut in, more to hurry the sad story along than anything else.

"Yes. So I went to the bordello. Auggie didn't look like herself. Fancy red dress, reeked with perfume, dusting powder, rouge on her cheeks, lips painted red. Auggie was a fallen woman. She said it was fun."

"You made allowances for your childhood friend." Fargo made it a flat statement, not a question.

Grace nodded. "Yes, I did. You see, Mr. Fargo, the holy Bible gives whores a profile same as it does for Satan. If David, whom the Lord dearly loved, and

Bathsheba committed adultery, then who am I to say it was wrong?

"Anyhow, Miss St. Claire taught Auggie to speak French, and Auggie taught me. We met under a mulberry out back of the bordello once a week. After two years under that mulberry, I knew French."

"What happened to Auggie?" Fargo wondered aloud.

"She kept working for two more years. I'd go visit her now and then. One day I went into Pascagoula and saw the charred remains of Miss St. Claire's bordello. I found her in a shrimp-boat captain's shack."

"Auggie?"

"No. Miss St. Claire. Mad as hell, I might add. She told me Auggie had robbed her, then blew up the bordello."

Fargo's brow furrowed.

"There's more. Auggie also robbed Skeeter's Saloon and old man Highsmith's bank. She blew up both of them, too."

"They hanged Auggie?"

"No. Auggie got away. No one in Pascagoula, including me, her best friend, ever saw Auggie again. I went to our elm to grieve and find solace. While praying for Auggie, God spoke to me from the creek."

"Was the creek on fire?" Fargo couldn't resist needling.

"No, Mr. Fargo, it wasn't anything like the burning bush. The creek gurgled His voice. God told me to rise, go forth, and take His word to lost sheep out on the frontier. Woe be it unto me to disobey God. I didn't want to become a pillar of salt or struck blind."

"It's a big frontier. Have you covered most of it?"

"Lord, no. I've been to only a fraction of it."

"Well, Grace, when we get to the gorge, I'll make these Irishmen uncapture you." He shot her a wink.

"You can pick back up on your crusade to bring in little lost sheep."

"You fun, Mr. Fargo. The Lord's work is serious business. That's why I can't continue the crusade."

"Oh? You want to explain that? And I wasn't funning."

Grace looked surprised as she answered, "Mr. Fargo, after last night I'm no different than these girls. That changed my life forevermore. It made me just like Auggie. Auggie was right, but I didn't believe her."

"Right? About what?"

"Auggie told me that once a man took my virginity, I would either hate all men or love them and want more."

"Uh, which is it? Love or hate?"

"I want more. I can't get it off my mind now that I know. I can't continue the crusade because I would be a self-righteous hypocrite. I can't preach against sin. I would stare at the men's groins and wonder how much they had. And they would see and know."

Before Fargo could reply, Wee Willie reined to a halt. The Irishman shouted, "Aw, shit!"

Fargo galloped to see the problem. All the wagons had rounded the bend. Here the canyon floor widened dramatically. A lengthy straightaway existed to the next bend. Erosion had carved mammoth cavernlike grooves in the walls. And a whiskey keg stood dead-center on the trail in front of the chuck wagon. The big man rode to the keg and dismounted. As he did, a tom-tom started to beat slowly. He ignored the sound and picked up the keg. It was empty, light as a feather. He tossed it off the trail. Waving the wagons forward, he scanned down the canyon to spot the Ute.

Wee Willie groaned, "I'm scared shitless."

Fargo glanced at him. Wee Willie quaked like an entire aspen grove. Fargo saw true fright in Wee Willie's widened, nervous eyes. "Come on, Wee Willie," he said in a soothing tone. "Slap those reins. There's nothing for you to get sick about. They left the keg for a refill. Chief Crossed-Eyes wants whiskey, not scalps." Fargo eased into his saddle.

Reluctantly, Wee Willie set the team to moving. Again, he groaned, "I'm still scared."

Fargo could believe that. "All right, Wee Willie, I'll ride ahead and shoo the Ute away. In case I miss them, this canyon is wide enough for you to circle the wagons should they attack."

Wee Willie watched the black-and-white pinto stallion trot ahead.

The Trailsman scanned all around for the Ute. While he heard the tom-tom, its sound seemed to come from everywhere. He decided the huge, half-tubes carved into the canyon walls were the cause. The echo-box effect made the single tom-tom sound like a dozen or more.

The female's piercing screams jerked Fargo's head around. He instantly knew what triggered the shrill outburst: the Ute were attacking from the rear. Wee Willie was already turning the chuck wagon to set up a defensive circle. As the Ute stormed around the bend behind the wagons, Fargo charged to join the swiftly forming circle. The hard-running Ovaro beat the Indians to the wagons. Fargo withdrew his Sharps from its saddle case and slid off his saddle as he reined the stallion to a halt inside the circle.

Half-naked, war-painted Ute warriors began circling the wagons. They whooped and hollered, swung their pogamoggans, shook tomahawks, fired carbines into the air, and shot arrows over the wagons. Fargo held his fire. He knew the Ute would not dare lower their aims for fear they would rupture a keg of firewater. The echo chamber fairly reverberated from all the loud gunfire. The women gathered in the middle of the circle to scream. The Irishmen lay doubled up on the ground next to the safe side of wagon wheels. Fargo stood and fired now and then over the warrior's heads, to intimidate them more than anything else.

It went on and on until the Ute ponies tired and halted. The warriors tried their best to keep their mounts circling, but the animals were too exhausted. Finally the warriors gave up trying to make them run. All shooting ceased. The Ute simply sat and stared at the kegs. Chief Crossed-Eyes dismounted. He tied a white rag to the crooked end of his war staff, then held the staff high and waved it as he walked toward the wagons.

Fargo went out to meet him. Fargo gave him the universal peace sign.

The chief had to squint and cock his head in order for his crossed eyes to see just one sign. In perfect English he said, "What's with the peace sign? We are at war. The next round we start killing and taking scalps. Yours first." Crossed-Eyes shifted weight onto his other foot. He growled, "Unless, of course, you part with the whiskey." He glanced up at Fargo and grinned.

"Aw, hell, Chief, why did you go and say that? You Ute are supposed to be friendly cusses."

"No, paleface," Crossed-Eyes snapped. "Not when it comes to whiskey. Are you going to give us some, or do I have to sic Ooompapa on you?"

Fargo focused on the row of mounted warriors behind their chief. His gaze settled on an unusually tall and muscular warrior. He decided he was looking at Ooompapa. Fargo didn't intend to brawl with a man brandishing an unusually big pogamoggan. He said, "Take one keg."

"Ha! Not when we can take all of them."

Fargo closed the gap separating them by one full

pace. With their noses touching, Fargo whispered, "Two kegs. That's my final offer. Take it or leave it."

A tense moment passed at a snail's pace. Finally Crossed-Eyes right hand shot out to Fargo's. The chief pumped Fargo's hand firmly one time, then said, "Deal! You drive a hard bargain, paleface." He motioned two warriors forward and grunted instructions to them.

They rode to a whiskey wagon. Each took a keg, then rode back and joined their companions.

Crossed-Eyes turned and headed for his horse.

Fargo called out to him, "And don't come back for refills. Hear that, old man?"

The chief didn't break stride. He grunted, ripped the white rag off his staff, threw it onto the ground, then booted it sky-high.

Fargo watched him get on his horse and lead the warriors into the shade below a stretch of overhang, where they dismounted to sit in a circle around the two kegs. When they started passing the kegs around, Fargo ordered the women and Irishmen to return to their wagons and head out.

A sour expression formed on Fools Gold's face. He said just as sourly, "You're giving away all our Irish whiskey."

"Shut up, Fools Gold," Fargo barked. "It's a small price to pay in exchange for keeping your scalps." Mounting up, he rode to scout ahead.

He rounded the far bend in midafternoon. A short stretch, more or less much the same as the longer one he'd just left, greeted him. Another bend prevented him from seeing what lay around it. He checked behind to see if the wagons were coming. Wee Willie had given the lead to Blinky O'Brien. Fargo waited for Blinky to catch up, then he rode to the next bend and halted. He saw two disturbing things: a length of gently weaving canyon narrowed severely, and the

71

leading edge of towering black thunderheads above the ridges at the far end of the canyon.

"Now I know why they call it Worser Canyon," Fargo told his horse.

The stallion knickered.

Not only was the canyon narrow, its walls slanted inward. He saw four places where the tops almost touched. The archlike configuration appeared fragile as all hell, dangerous and ready to collapse at any moment. Fargo did not want to pass under the arches, but there was no possible way for him to go around them.

He looked at the dark thunderheads. Shortly they would bring lightning bolts and booming thunder. Either one could cause an arch to fall. If the wagons were under one when that happened, they would be buried under tons of rocks. Fargo shuddered at the thought. He waited for the wagons to arrive.

He halted the procession and told the drivers to gather around him. When they were there, he said, "Folks, I don't like the looks of this stretch in the canyon. Those arches can crash down from the weakest of jolts. I want you drivers to spread out. Keep enough distance between the wagons so if an arch does fall, it will flatten only the one unlucky enough to be caught under it. Now, I don't have to tell you to hurry when you pass beneath the arches. I'll ride ahead and watch for trouble."

"I'm scared shitless," Wee Willie groaned.

"Me, too," agreed O'Malley.

Blinky added, "I never saw those arches before now."

Gotcheye claimed, "Me neither."

"I ain't coming this way no more," Fools Gold stated emphatically.

They all nodded.

Fargo looked at Can Can.

She shrugged.

Fargo ordered them back to the wagons. When they were seated, he motioned them forward, then rode ahead. The air was deathly still. A hush fell over the canyon. The Ovaro seemed to sense the latent danger. The big man looked up at the lower surface of the arch as he passed under it. Suddenly a piece of rock broke loose. It barely made a sound. The piece of jagged-edged stone wedged into a chink of a larger rock, much like a perfect fit in a jigsaw puzzle. Fargo exhaled. The Ovaro walked on. Only after clearing the danger did the big man look behind.

Blinky drove the lead wagon. Gotcheye followed him. The tarts came next. The twins and jenny were close beside the tart wagon. They blocked his view, prevented him from seeing the order of the other three wagons. Not that it mattered. They would either make it safely through Worser Canyon or they would not. It occurred to Fargo an arch would collapse in advance of the lead wagon. Tons of rock would dam the canyon, effectively separating him from the wagons. And that thought spawned another worse than the first: what if two arches fell and trapped all the wagons between them? He shook his head to clear that thought.

The dark, ugly clouds blotted the sun. A cool breeze came down the canyon, smacked his face, riffled his hair. Fargo cleared his throat when he heard a low roll of thunder. Soon, lightning flashed in the clouds. The evening storm would arrive momentarily. Through the rapidly fading light, the big man strained to scan the third arch. It was one where the two edges of the walls curved and nearly touched. Fargo believed he could easily step across the gap that separated the two stone curvatures.

As he passed slowly beneath the arch, the breeze strengthened to a stiff wind. Close on the heels of the wind, an eerie sort of darkness filled Worser Canyon. Lightning flashed. It seemed to laugh at the big man astride the magnificent black-and-white pinto stallion. Thunder boomed and rumbled down the canyon. Fargo glanced up at the arch. The thunder hadn't disturbed it.

Rain pelted the big man as he rode between the third and fourth archways. Roiling, low-hanging clouds covered the entire canyon. Total darkness fell. The stiff wind changed to gale force. With that change in strength, the witch started to wail. The shrieking cry sent a chill down Fargo's spine. A massive bolt of lightning stabbed downward behind him. The resulting mighty roar of thunder instantly followed. The ground shook.

Fargo turned in the saddle to check on the wagons. Can Can's wagon was approaching the third archway. Within seconds she would be directly underneath it. Fargo paused to watch her.

As he did, a bolt of lightning struck the top of the arch. The arch glowed blue-white, but not one rock fell. Instead, he saw ropes dangling, much like tendrils from the arch.

And men were sliding down the ropes.

6

The Trailsman drew his Colt, wheeled the Ovaro, and rushed to the rescue. Passing Blinky, Fargo shouted, "Run for your life. Hurry." Passing Gotcheye, he sounded the same warning.

Between the witch's shrieking the tarts' and twins' screaming, and the jenny's panic-stricken hee-haws, Fargo lost all sense of direction and rode past the tart wagon completely. He didn't realize the error until lightning flashed and he saw O'Malley staring wide-eyed at him. Of his own accord, the Ovaro skidded to a halt in front of O'Malley's team. Fargo turned the stallion and rode back to the tart wagon.

He heard a sharp cracking sound behind him, then a crash. The witch's wail ceased abruptly. Fargo knew the second arch had collapsed, blocking passage through the canyon.

In the darkness and wind-driven rain blinding him, Fargo homed in on the women's screams. Through their screams he heard a new sound: a tuba. Distinctly, he heard it repeatedly making the same sound: ooompapa, ooompapa, ooompapa. "Surely I'm mistaken," he muttered to himself.

Lightning flashed. He counted twelve burly men running helter-skelter away from the tart wagon, dragging resisting females behind them. Other men tried to catch women fleeing on the ground. One of the men, a huge fellow, dragged a woman, who Fargo thought was Charleen, by the hair on her head. He made the ooompapa tubalike sound.

Fargo had to make a choice: rescue the running females, or go after the draggers. He decided on the former. He would get to the latter later. He dismounted and bent to the task.

When he tackled a burly fellow about to snatch a tart, the man yelped, *"Achtung!"* Fargo pulled him to his feet and slammed his right fist into the fellow's face. Bone crunched. The man fell unconscious. Fargo told the tart to return to the wagon, then settled on the next man.

He too, cried, *"Achtung!"* just before Fargo threw a haymaker that powered against the left side of the man's head. Sucking his skinned knucks, Fargo told the tart to go back to the wagon. He looked around to spot his next victim.

Altogether he caught and knocked out six of the burly men. All cried the same thing: *achtung*. He went to the tart wagon and waited for lightning to flash so he could see whom he rescued. The twins and Grace were missing. One of the burly men had a fighting hellcat on his hands—Charleen Bodner. Charleen would resist until she took her dying breath.

Mounting up, Fargo told Can Can to catch up with Blinky's wagon, that he would be along shortly with Grace and the twins. Of course Can Can didn't understand one word of what he said. Fargo had to use hand signals to make the woman move forward and pass through the ropes.

Fargo had seen the men drag the women toward the second archway, which had collapsed and now blocked the canyon. He rode that way through blinding rain.

Fargo rode a lazy S pattern to grope his way through the vicious night storm. By the time he reached the newly created rock barricade, he hadn't seen or heard the women. He stared through the torrential downpour at the ten-foot-high pile of rocks and boulders, knowing he would have to climb them, knowing a fight awaited him on the far side. Fargo sighed heavily. Dismounting, he muttered under his breath, "Women! They're more trouble than they're worth."

Standing atop the stone dam, he waited for lightning to flash and light up the narrow canyon floor. When it accommodated him, Fargo saw the three couples wallowing in the mud. He eased down the rocks and went to them. The huge man lay between one of the twins thighs. His big butt rose and fell in cadence with his ooompapas. Charlene's struggle to escape was useless under the man's heavy weight. Grace squirmed under the weight of her burly man and moaned.

Popping his knuckles, Fargo said, "All right, boys, that's enough screwing for one night. You can make it easy on yourself by walking away, or hard by tangling with me. Which do you prefer?"

Fargo nudged Ooompapa's big butt with the toe of his right boot. "Get off Charleen."

Ooompapa fired up his mouth tuba. He rose slowly and hitched up his pants. Cracking his knuckles, Ooompapa glowered at Fargo and growled, *"Achtung!"*

The other two burly men echoed, *"Achtung!"* They, too, arose.

The brawl began.

Ooompapa grabbed Fargo and put a bear hug on him.

The other two burly men pounded Fargo's back.

The women sat in the swirling muddy water and watched.

Fargo managed to land a solid punch on Ooompapa's jaw.

Ooompapa sucked in a breath and shoved Fargo back.

Fargo staggered against one of the burly men. The man fell and splattered into the mud. Fargo drove a fist into Ooompapa's belly. Ooompapa absorbed the powerful blow without so much as a grunt. Fargo knew he had one tough son of a bitch on his hands. He spun and looped another uppercut to the other burly man's square jaw, then planted a boot heel in the face of the one in the mud.

Fargo ducked a power-laden punch to the head thrown by Ooompapa. Off-balance, Ooompapa caught a hard right in the right eye jabbed by Fargo. Ooompapa reeled. Fargo followed up with a fast left and right to the huge man's shaggy head. Ooompapa sunk to his knees. Fargo turned to take on the other two. He saw the big cowards had fled into the rainy night.

He entwined his fingers in Ooompapa's unruly hair, positioned the huge man's head just so, then delivered his best knockout punch. When he released his grip on the burly man's hair, Ooompapa fell facedown into the muddy water.

The females applauded the big man's performance.

Fargo looked at them and said, "Where's your clothes? Put them on. Get back to the wagons. Make it snappy." He strode for the rocky barrier.

He sat easy in his saddle while waiting for them. Naked Maureen appeared first. She explained her nudity. "Fargo, those burly men ripped off our clothes first thing. We don't know where our clothes are."

As Maureen spoke, Charleen and Grace came down the rocks. He grunted, "Damn! I'll miss my duster." Strengthening his voice, he told them to keep close to the Ovaro while walking back to the wagons.

Fargo grimaced as he scanned the naked females. With a sigh he said, "All right, ladies, everyone get in or under the tart wagon. Grace, you tell them what I said."

"I'm cold," Grace whined.

"Brrr! Me too," added a twin.

"Me, too. Brrr," reverse-echoed the other.

"So?" questioned Fargo.

Grace said, "Put your arms around me. Hug me tight."

The jenny hee-hawed.

Fargo started rounding up Irishmen. He told each to meet him at the tart wagon. Fargo and Wee Willie carried the canvas. The big man made a canvas shelter, a lean-to of sorts, over the bed of the tart wagon.

"This thing leaks," Charleen bitched. "We might as well be standing in the rain."

"Suit yourself," Fargo replied. He climbed over the side of the wagon and sat with his back to the driver's seat.

The others quickly followed. The tarts and Irishmen paired up. Maureen and Grace snuggled up against Fargo. Charleen sat alone at the rear of the wagon. Fargo gave them time to get reasonably comfortable, then said, "Okay, O'Malley, who were those burly men?"

"Ooompapa?"

"That his name?"

"That's what we call him. He goes around making that sound all the time. We call them the achtungers. They're Germans. Like these tarts, here, don't any of them speak a lick of English. All they say is *achtung*. They have a mine a short distance from here. Over by the Skull and Crossbones mine."

"This has happened before?" Fargo intoned.

O'Malley nodded. "Uh, huh. Ever year the achtungers come down those ropes. Ever year they beat us up and steal all the whiskey they can carry off. But

79

this time was different. They must have smelled pussy in the wind and rain."

"Or the pirates told them." Fargo mused aloud.

"First the Ute," Fargo began, "then the rogues, now the achtungers. All after your whiskey. In the past, seems to me as though you boys got home with empty wagons. Why do you bother hauling kegs of whiskey all the way from Denver just to let them take it away from you?"

O'Malley mumbled sheepishly, "We keep thinking, them being on foot and all, they might miss seeing us, then we could get a load through. You'd think our wagons could outrun 'em, but they don't. Them pirates and achtungers are fast runners."

"Then, what you're saying is, you have never got to Blood Gorge with a load of whiskey. That right, O'Malley?"

"Not one keg," he admitted. "We had to suffer all through the winter with nary a drop to warm our insides."

Fargo shook his head. "I guess you know those overhanging walls caving in means you boys are making your last whiskey run from Denver?"

All the Irishmen put glum expressions on their faces. They nodded in unison. O'Malley asked hopefully, "Do you think you can get us through? We need this load of winter whiskey real bad."

Fargo would sure as hell try. He said, "Hope so. What lies ahead?"

"Meadowlark Meadow. It's a long narrow meadow. Takes a whole day to cross it. Then comes Mean Canyon. There's a big pond in Meadowlark. We always stop at the pond to scrub off."

"How far is it to the meadow?"

"In this storm and mud? Oh, I'd say 'bout sunup. If we leave now."

"Then we best head out. I want out of Worser Canyon as fast as possible. The achtungers and pirates might come back." Fargo moved to leave the wagon.

Grace spoke briefly to the tarts. The tarts smiled, nodded. Oui Oui said her name. Can Can said, "Can Can can." Déjà Vu moaned,"*Déjà vu.*" Mimi squealed gleefully. Ooolala rolled her eyes back, went, "Ooolala."

Grace explained, "We have agreed to be sacrificial lambs. This Irish whiskey must get through at all costs, otherwise these poor men won't make it through the cold, brutal winter. Leave us here for those sex-starved poor rogues and burly men to take. We will suffer for the cause."

"What about us?" Maureen or Charleen asked.

"Yeah, you redheaded, big-busted, mattress-thrasher," Charleen hissed, as only she could. "Sacrificial lambs, indeed. Hunh!"

Fargo paused from dropping to the ground. He briefly considered leaving all the females behind, then thought of Miss Precious Goodbody and how much relief they could give her. He said, "No one or anything gets left behind. I'm taking you people and this good Irish whiskey to Blood Gorge. And that's final. I don't want to hear another word about sacrificing. And that, too, is final. Now, you Irishmen take your seats and start rolling." Fargo pressed over the side.

Thunder boomed. Lightning flashed.

7

Fargo mounted up and rode to the fourth archway. He reined to a halt and swung the Ovaro around to put his rump to the wind-driven rain. As the second and subsequent wagons crept past him, he told the drivers to close up. After Wee Willie's chuck wagon, the last in the column, went by him, he rode to the tart wagon, dismounted, and trailed the twins' horses and jenny behind it. He knew the Ovaro would keep him in sight, alert and ready for action on a split second's notice, so he didn't bother to trail him. Fargo climbed up in the driver's seat and took the reins from Can Can. He gestured the shivering, nude whore to get under the canvas with the others. After a long moment of silence, he began chatting over his shoulder with Grace and the twins.

"Did you ladies lose all your clothes?"

Grace answered, "Yes, Mr. Fargo. Those burly men ripped them first thing and flung them away. Whatever will we do?"

Charleen replied, "Grace Hatfield, your nasty body won't see any of my clothing, or my sister's. So don't ask."

"I'll go naked like the others," Maureen allowed. "I'm saving my change of clothes until all this is over. I don't want to ride into Tucson without a stitch on."

"Weren't you afraid, Charleen?" Fargo asked.

"Humph," she snorted. "I did what I had to do.

Those men were huge and stronger than me. You are being paid to protect me and my sister, and you didn't do it. We were forced to look out for ourselves, no thanks to you."

"Skye did the best he could," Maureen said in his defense.

"Yes, look at it this way," Grace added. "We held those burly men down until Fargo could get there."

Fargo chuckled. Grace had a point. He obliquely changed the subject. "What makes you think I will get you to Tucson?"

"Oh? What makes you think you won't?" Charleen snapped.

"Snow."

Grace gasped, "*Snow?* Is it snowing, Fargo, darling?"

"Not yet. But it will. Soon. Sooner than you think. I smell snow in the wind."

"You're lying, Mr. Fargo," Charleen said. "You can't smell snow. No one can. You're just trying to scare us. I know your kind. The first flake of snow you see, you will keep our money and abandon us. You're rotten to the core, Mr. Fargo. I've said it all along."

"No, Sis, you're wrong about Skye," Maureen censured. "He's an honorable man. Skye keeps his word. Don't you, Skye?"

"I keep my promises," Fargo agreed. "When the time comes, I'll ask three times if you two want to back out. However, I might not get the chance."

"Oh, why not?" Grace interrupted.

"Because of the German or pirate miners," Fargo explained. "They are tenacious bastards, ones who don't give up easily. I'm already black and blue from fighting them. One more assault and I daresay I won't be able to fend them off. If I can't, they will capture and take you women to their mine."

"See! What did I tell you?" Charleen hissed. "He's planning to throw us to the wolves. He's just hoping and praying those evil men will come back. When they do, you will see the big coward slink away. Black and blue, my ass! Mr. Fargo, you don't have a mark on your body."

Maureen mused, "Oh, Sis, he does, too. Darling, Skye is no sissy. Why, he's black and blue all over. Isn't that right, Skye, darling?"

While he hadn't actually inspected his body, he believed it was bruised in several places. He muttered defensively, "Blue-blackbeard all but chewed off one of my ears."

"See, Sis?" Maureen sighed. "What did I tell you? The poor man's hurt."

Charleen retaliated. Venomously, she said, "La-dee-da. He got his ear nibbled while I nearly got stabbed to death."

Grace said, "Wasn't it thrilling?"

"You can shut up, Grace Hatfield," Charleen barked. "You may have enjoyed wallowing with those foul-smelling men, but my sister and I did not."

"Speak for yourself, Sis," Maureen suggested.

And that ended the testy conversation. Fargo drove into the rain and kept his thoughts private. Mostly he thought about the hunger pains growling in his stomach. If it was a sunny day over Meadowlark Valley, he reckoned he would bag a deer and have Wee Willie cook it while he bathed in the pond. After satisfying his hunger, he would spread his bedroll and catch a nap.

Dawn came late, due to storm clouds. The downpour changed to a steady drizzle when the wagons rolled out of Worser Canyon. The dark clouds raced overhead, moving the thunder and lightning away. Fargo listened to it rumble and fade down the length of the canyon. The sky lightened. Shortly thereafter the drizzle ceased. Holes appeared in the trailing edge of the clouds. The sun peeked through. Then, as though done by magic, the last vestige of the storm vanished and left the long, wet valley glistening in a rainbow of late fall colors.

At Fargo's distance from the mountains on either side of the great meadow, the forests of conifers and the irregular contours of the mountains blended and left the illusion of being a flat, unbroken plane. The ever-changing angle of the sun painted this otherwise-green sameness in ever-changing tints and hues, tones and shades of lighter or darker greens. Here and there streaks of golden beauty speared partway up the green mountainsides. And when the angle of the sun crept into the right position, for a fleeting moment its rays added a splash of pretty blue when they kissed on blue spruce. Three snow-capped mountain peaks sparkled diamondlike under the bright sun.

The floor of the meadow—also green, but a different shade, much lighter—was dotted with ferns and fall wildflowers that grew in profusion. Up close they stood out. Fargo recognized a few types of the wildflowers as he rode through them: pasqueflower, blue columbine, bell-shaped sego lily, globe anemone. Broad-tailed hummingbirds hovered at and poked their needle-pointed, long beaks into blue-and-white five-petaled Colorado blue columbine. Five tree swallows flew low over the meadow in front of the wagons, heading toward aspen in the west. As the grass, ferns, and wildflowers reached outward, farther and farther away from Fargo, they, too, blended, and much like an artist's palette became a rush of ill-defined colors.

For the moment the Trailsman relished in nature's glory. Under different circumstances he would have lingered here and been immersed in the beauty of it all. As Fargo listened to the monotonous plodding of the team's hooves and the creaking and groaning of the wagon wheels, his thoughts drifted to the realities of his present situation. He wondered how in the hell he got into it in the first place. If he had arrived in Powderhorn a day later, he argued with himself, he would have missed Maureen Bodner altogether. The woman represented an anchor. He was tied to it, and her, until he reached Tucson.

If that wasn't bad enough, the domino effect swiftly followed. Crazy Utes, crazier latter-day pirates, ooom-papaing Germans, not to mention bitchy Charleen and a fallen crusader, plus a wagonload of French tarts, whom he did not understand, and a bunch of crazier Irishmen tumbled into his path.

When will it end? he asked himself. Maureen Bodner and her twin were more trouble than they were worth, especially Charleen. The nasty-tempered female was a burr under his saddle. At least, he sighed, a measure of relief will come after we arrive in Blood Gorge. Then I'll have to contend with only the two of them. Thank God for that, he mused. Fargo grimaced as he raised his eyes and looked ahead. Behind, he heard the females stir and begin chattering in low, sleepy tones.

The women took down and folded the canvas, then sun-dried their bodies. Fargo looked over his shoulder at them. They sat with their eyes closed, their faces tilted to the warm sun. Never before had Fargo seen this much nudity, and all of it was on shapely bodies. The jostle of the wagon caused their breasts to bounce and jiggle, especially Grace Hatfield's. She had the largest pair. In her relaxed position, they swayed to and fro. The areolae were soft-brown and as big as silver dollars. The tiny nipples protruded proudly. A sun ray kissed the left one as it swayed into the correct angle to catch the kiss. For an instant, the damp nipple and areola sparkled.

Grace opened one eye. It looked straight into Fargo's gaze. Arching her back slightly, Grace winked and smiled wickedly. She held the naughty smile, but closed her eye.

Fargo sensed the woman had just set a trap. He looked forward, over the twins' backs. In the far distance rose a tall outcrop partially surrounded by thickets. Beyond the thickets a grove of golden aspen shimmered in the breeze.

Blinky hollered, "Hey, Fargo! You want to stop at the pond, or keep on going?"

"Stop at the pond," he called back.

Fargo halted next to the gap in the outcrop. He dropped to the ground and walked through the gap. The outcrop ringed the small spring-fed pond, the thicket grew immediately east of the rocks. A short distance separated the thicket from an aspen grove.

Gotcheye and Can Can appeared behind Fargo. Gotcheye said, "Nice pond, isn't it? Ice-cold, too."

The calm water was crystal-clear. Fargo watched several springs bubble sand on the bottom. The overflow traced into the outcrop's south rim. "Beautiful, in fact," Fargo answered, almost whispering. "Hell is separated by beauty and serenity." He nodded toward Worser Canyon to emphasize the statement. Then he turned and walked to his horse.

Fargo mounted up and rode around the outcrop and thicket one time. He watched the ground for deer paths and saw two. Both connected the pond to the mountains framing Meadowlark Valley. He halted at the chuck wagon, where the Irishmen had gathered. The women were at the pond. He heard them talking. The Irishmen were sullen, sluggish. He told them, "Boys, don't get nervous when you see me ride away. I'm going to shoot us some red meat. Be back shortly. Wee Willie, have a hot fire when I get back."

Wee Willie nodded.

O'Malley muttered, "I don't think you ought to leave us unprotected and all."

Fargo scanned the length and breadth of the pretty valley. "Trevor, there isn't a soul in sight. They're not coming back."

Fools Gold mumbled, "That's what you say."

Fargo did not know what he was going to do with this bunch of Irishmen. They were born worriers. He wished one of them, just one, would express an optimistic attitude. They were the kind that would look at a glass half-filled with whiskey and say it was half-empty. Fargo's shoulders sagged. He shook his head slowly. He sighed heavily, then said, "I'll keep an eye open for trouble. Build the fire, Wee Willie. I'll want coffee when I return." He reined the Ovaro toward the deer path leading to the aspen and nudged him into a walk.

Midway to the grove, he heard Maureen shout, "Where are you going, Skye, darling?"

He glanced behind. Maureen and two tarts stood on pinnacles of the outcrop, their milk-white, nude bodies in stark contrast to the dark-green foliage on the mountainside rising in the distance behind them. He waved, but didn't answer.

Fargo followed the deer path into the aspen grove, where he saw scratch marks on several tree trunks— sure signs of cougars sharpening their claws. He noticed one set of marks were fresh; the tree sap still glistened in the elongated gashes.

The single deer path ended a short distance on the far side of the grove. It divided into three smaller paths. All led into the blue-spruce forest growing on the mountainside. He chose to follow the middle path.

Fresh deer droppings and deer prints led him up the mountainside to a rocky overhang. Knowing he was close to the herd, he eased off the saddle and withdrew his Sharps from its saddle case. Then he hugged the inner surface of the overhang until he reached the end of it. Fargo peered around a boulder. Two plump doe lay sunning themselves in a patch of grass easy shots from his distance. He bypassed them. Fargo wanted the buck. He knew the buck would be near the doe, standing alert, vigilant to imminent danger. His gaze scanned all around the pair of doe. He spotted two others nibbling grass among the blue spruce. He raised his vision and swept the area behind the grazing doe.

As the Trailsman's keen eyesight moved among the trees, he glimpsed the buck all but hidden by two trees. The buck stood on a ledge overlooking the doe. Fargo reckoned fifty yards separated him from the buck. He raised the Sharps ever so slowly and brought it into position to fire a killing shot. Focusing on the buck's heart area, he began applying pressure on the trigger. As it was supposed to do, his gradual squeeze fired the rifle without him anticipating the explosion or a kick.

Two things happened simultaneously: through the wisp of gunsmoke curling at the end of the rifle barrel he saw the buck flinch from the bullet's impact, and he felt claws dig into the skin on his back.

The cougar's weight knocked Fargo to the ground. Man and deadly beast were one as they tumbled down the mountainside locked in a death struggle. In the spiraling blur of his vision, Fargo glimpsed the trunk of a lodgepole pine rushing at him. He twisted his back, with the cougar fused tightly on it, to the trunk. The lodgepole shook when it knocked the cougar off the big man's back. Fargo skidded a few feet farther. Scrambling to his feet, he whipped his Colt from its holster.

But the cougar leapt before he could fire, and knocked the Colt out of his grasp. Instinctively, the big cat tried to pull its victim to the ground. Bracing himself on the incline, Fargo grabbed the cougar's throat and held its flesh-ripping teeth away from his face. The cat dug its claws into Fargo's shoulders, twisted its head violently to wrench free from the big man's choking grip on its throat.

As he struggled to maintain his balance, Fargo willed himself to ignore the pain in his shoulders. Inch by slow inch he pushed the cougar's opened jaws further away from his throat. His biceps became steellike; he sweated profusely and gritted his teeth as he forced back the bared teeth.

Straining with all his might, Fargo wrenched the cougar from his body. For an instant he held it at arm's length. His arms quivered under the heavy pendulum of the cougar's thrashing body. Calling upon a reserve of strength, Fargo began twirling. Momentum brought the snarling cat up. After two fast revolutions, Fargo release his grip. The cougar slammed into a tree trunk.

Fargo snatched his Arkansas toothpick from its calf sheath. He attacked the stunned cougar. The stiletto blade flashed four times, three dripping blood. The fifth time he stabbed, the slender blade pierced the big cat's heart, and he left the knife buried hilt-deep in the flesh.

He steadied himself on the lodgepole tree while he watched the dead cougar's body jerk. Finally, he whistled to the Ovaro. The stallion came to him. Fargo removed his canteen from the saddlehorn, rinsed his mouth out, then sloshed the rest of the cool water on his cuts. He retrieved his three weapons. Only then did he look up at the ledge to see if he dropped the buck. He wasn't sure, but he thought he had. The clump of undergrowth hanging over the ledge might have camouflaged the buck's rack.

Fargo climbed into his saddle and went to check. The buck wasn't on the ledge, but his blood was. Fargo followed the buck's bloody path of flight until he found him sprawled on another ledge. He dismounted and lifted the buck's head. Fargo had bagged a ten-pointer. He bent to the task of gutting his prize. Thirty minutes later, Fargo rode down the mountainside, the buck draped behind him.

The Irishmen walked out to meet him. When they saw his tattered, blood-splotched buckskin shirt, their eyes widened and their jovial expressions wilted to concern.

Fargo explained, "Me and a cougar tangled," and let it go at that.

At the chuck wagon, they helped him remove the buck. He told Wee Willie to skin the deer and have roast venison ready when he got back.

"Er, you going somewhere, again?" Wee Willie asked nervously.

"Not far," Fargo replied. He began unsaddling and taking everything off the Ovaro. While he did, he looked around for the women.

Blinky noticed. He explained, "They're in the rocks. Either bathing or catching some sun."

Fargo nodded. "I'll chase them out." He led the stallion to the outcrop.

Maureen and four tarts sunned themselves on the scant banks of the pond. Charleen and the other two tarts were neck-deep in the water. He didn't see Grace.

Maureen opened her eyes and asked, "What are you going to do with that pretty horse, Skye, darling?"

"Give him a bath. What else?"

"Not in this pool, you're not," Charleen announced curtly. "Not while I'm in it."

Fargo ignored her. He pulled off his boots and socks, stood them on a flat rock, then removed his hat and neckerchief and sat them on top of his boots.

The tarts watched fascinated.

Maureen grinned naughtily and purred, "It's show-time at the pond."

Charleen demanded, "What do you think you're doing, exposing yourself to us? I knew you would get around to doing it sooner or later. Get out of here, Mr. Fargo, and take your filthy horse with you."

As though she had cued him, the powerful stallion's long member unsheathed.

Charleen blasted out of the water and ran through the gap. The wide-eyed tarts exchanged glances, commenced chattering back and forth in excited tones of voice. Fargo pulled his shirt off.

Maureen came to her feet at once. She winced from the sight of so many scratches. A hand flew to her mouth. She gasped, "Oh, Fargo, what happened?"

"It's a long story. I don't want to talk about it."

The twin started coming toward him. Fargo knew what she wanted. He didn't intend to let her love him in pretense of taking care of his wounds. His upraised hand stopped her. "Maureen, I'm in no mood to play with you. You best leave the outcrop. Go help Wee Willie prepare the venison." He waved the tarts out of the water. They were more obedient than Maureen, who left only after pausing twice to strike provocative poses, which he ignored.

The Ovaro knickered. Fargo braced against the pinto's left withers to remove the calf sheath and stiletto, the blade of which he inspected. Finding a trace of crusted blood at the handle, he flipped the stiletto toward a sandy spot on the bank. The knife stabbed in the sand blade first. He encouraged the stallion to enter the water. The Ovaro knickered lowly, rumbling, as though conveying to his master that the water was damn frigid. Fargo chuckled, took his gun belt off, then his Levi's and underdrawers. Taking a deep breath, he dived in and swam underwater to the far bank. Breaking the surface, he gasped, "Cold, isn't it, boy?"

A throaty knicker came from the horse.

Grace's voice said, "Mr. Fargo, has anyone told you lately that you have a beautiful body?"

He glanced about to find her. Grace lay facedown atop the tallest boulder in the outcrop. Propped on one elbow, she looked straight at him and smiled.

"Not today," he offered.

She pushed up into a sitting position. As she did, her heavy breasts hung down to their fullest. Fargo became aroused immediately.

Grace said, "Well, I'm saying you do. Where'd you get all the scratches? Ooolala?"

He shook his head. "Cougar." He watched her stand and dive in. The near-perfect plunge hardly made ripples on the water.

She broke surface right in front of him. She, too, gasped, "Brrr! God, it is cold, ice-cold."

Fargo chuckled. "You want to help me wash the blood off my horse?" Grace nodded. Fargo told her to take the left side. "Horses don't like the smell of blood, especially when its on them," he explained. "So scrub him good."

The Ovaro stood still while they went about cleaning him. Finished, Fargo aimed the stallion at the gap and nudged him forward. The pinto left the water and paused in the gap to look behind at Fargo.

Grace murmured her appreciation, "God, but he's so beautiful. Gleaming jet-black fore- and hind-quarters, pure white midsection. Yeah, I'm talking about you, boy." She glanced at Fargo and asked, "How long have you had him?"

"Since the time he was born. I'm the only mother he knows. The mare died giving birth. I pulled him from her womb. We're inseparable, he and I. I rode a dun filly back then. He tagged alongside, followed me everywhere I went. When the time came, I saddled him and mounted up. He accepted the saddle and bit like a true gentleman. I didn't have to break him. It was as though he knew what was expected of him." Fargo strengthened his voice. "Go on, boy. Go graze."

Shaking his head, the powerful stallion trotted through the gap.

Grace said, "Let me look at those scratches. I see several are open gashes."

He put his back to her. "The only reason they are not worse," he began, "is because I was wearing my buckskin shirt. The thickness of it made the difference." He felt her fingers move along the wounds on his back and shoulders. As she felt, her tiny, rock-hard nipples grazed his skin occasionally. Fargo tried to ignore the sensuous sensation, but try as he may, he could not. He turned to face her. Their eyes met.

Grace whispered, "Take me, Fargo. Please take me, now."

He embraced her. They kissed openmouthed, her hot breathing and hotter, wet tongue exploring the inside of his mouth, his trying to corral it.

Grace Hatfield closed her eyes. Curling a slender arm around his neck, she moaned, "Oh, God, you taste wonderful . . . so wonderful." Her free hand lowered to his hard-on and gripped it. As she slowly stroked his manhood, her breathing quickened. She gasped, "Oh, God . . . I want to feel . . . you inside me. Please?"

He worked the two of them over to the shallow part of the pond. There wasn't room enough for them to lie on the sandy bank, so he laid her head and shoulders on it. Grace parted her legs. He got between them. She arched her back. The twin mounds punched partway out of the water. She gazed into his eyes and whispered, "Kiss them, Fargo. Nurse on them. And, oh, yes nibble on them."

As he rolled the left nipple between his teeth, he felt her fingers curl around his member. When he sucked in a mouthful of the pillowy breast, she squirmed, whimpering, "Oh, God, oh, God! That feels so good . . . so good. The other one, Fargo . . . suck it, too. Don't stop."

He slid to her right breast, nibbled the peaked nipple, then took in as much of the breast as his mouth would hold. Grace's head lolled. She began writhing wildly, twisting and turning, thrusting the breast harder and harder into his mouth. She mewed childlike, "I'm on fire. Yes, yes . . . I'm burning hot."

Fargo felt her touch his summit to her eager lower lips and then part them. She teased the slit by rubbing the head of his organ up and down through it, all the while moaning joyously, "Nice, nice . . . that feels so good, so very good."

Finally Grace positioned his blood-swollen crown for penetration. Her hands moved onto his hard buttocks, her legs up to his waist. Fargo entered slowly by half his length. Her eyes flew open as she gasped, "Oh, my God—oh, my God!" She continued to gasp the words until he was all the way in.

Fargo fused his base to her opening and commenced gyrating his hips slowly. Grace murmured through clenched teeth, "Oh, God, oh, my God, you're big. It's so heavy and filling. I'm in heaven. I know I am. More, Fargo, more, more, more."

Maintaining the gyration, he began thrusting in and out. Grace picked up on his rhythm, moved her hands onto his broad shoulders, and locked her ankles high on his waist. In the new position she was wide open for his deep plunges, and she started bucking to force them to happen.

Her fingernails added to the cougar's marks and signaled her forthcoming orgasm. She gasped, "My mouth . . . so dry. What's happening to me! Oh . . . oh, my God!"

Her velvety interior seized around him. She grunted, "Aaagh! What is happening down there? I'm seeing beautiful shooting stars."

When Fargo erupted, Grace screamed, "Aaaugh! Lordy, lordy, that's hot!"

Grace rolled onto her side, propped on an elbow. Drawing tiny circles on his chest and shoulders, she complimented, "You're the best I've ever had. You made me feel like a woman. Charleen Bodner was wrong about you."

"Wrong?" he mumbled.

"Yes. She said you were disgusting. You're not disgusting. Thrilling, exciting, yes, but not disgusting." Grace told him other hard words Charleen had to say about him.

But Fargo didn't hear them. Between the circling fingertip, the warm sun on his body, and her soft monotone drawl, it put him to sleep. But not for long. A wet kiss awakened him.

He looked into her eyes. "Grace, don't start something you can't finish," he muttered.

Grace rolled atop him. "I watched Mimi and a rogue do it this way last night. I don't know how. Show me."

Fargo showed her.

Afterward, they swam across the pond to his clothes. He handed her his cougar-tattered shirt. "Put it on. I have a spare."

She slipped the shirt over her head. The shirttail fell to her thighs. She struck a sensuous pose for him. Pulling on his underwear, he chuckled. "What's so funny?" she asked.

"You. If only the gang back in Powderhorn could see you now."

"Powderhorn?"

As he looked at her, it occurred to him that she crusaded in so many towns, villages, and hamlets on the frontier that they ran together. Grace the crusader didn't remember the names of any of them, or the faces of the people. He pulled on his Levi's, then his boots. But they remembered her, he told himself, and her preaching. He put on his gun belt, picked up his hat and neckerchief. In that regard, he continued the thought, she had given them pause to reflect. He said, "Powderhorn isn't important. Come on, high-toned woman. I smell venison."

The Irishmen, tarts, and a twin poked their heads from the tall grass where they lay. The other twin sat in the driver's seat of the chuck wagon. Fargo walked up to the fire. Wee Willie had skewered cuts of venison and stuck the ends of the skewers in the ground at an angle so the venison would catch the heat. Then left them that way while he frolicked with the tarts. The side facing the fire had burned to a crisp, the other left blood raw. And the coffee had boiled away.

Grace glanced from the skewers encircling the fire to the coffeepot, then him, and exclaimed, "Now that's what I call disgusting."

Nodding his agreement, he called out to the twin on the driver's seat, "Charleen or Maureen, get off that driver's seat and come here."

She replied tartly, "What do you want, Mr. Fargo? I'm tired."

"Charleen," muttered Grace.

"Why didn't you turn this venison?" Fargo called to her.

"I don't like deer meat," Charleen answered.

Disgusted, Fargo pulled a skewer out of the ground and took a bite of venison. He spit it out and dropped the rest onto the fire. "I nearly got killed getting that buck," he lamented. "And for what?"

Gotcheye's voice cried from the grass, "They're coming. They're coming fast!"

Fargo turned and looked in the direction of Gotcheye's point. Many riders pounded toward the wagons. They rode from the near end of Mean Canyon.

8

Fargo shouted to the Irishmen, "Everyone back to the wagons. Hurry." Moving to his saddle case, he checked to see if his Colt was fully loaded. He squinted at the horsemen as he withdrew his Sharps. They were still too far away and ill-defined for him to make out. He checked the rifle to make sure it was fully loaded.

The clumsy Irishmen and tarts reminded Fargo of the circus clowns he saw in Minneapolis back in '58. The Irishmen were hopping, one leg in and one leg out of their pants, trying to pull them up with one hand and getting on their shirts with the other. They reeled, staggered or stumbled, and fell while trying to dress on the run. The tarts were no help at all. Like the Irishmen, they were scared and confused. In their confusion they ran helter-skelter, paused briefly to assist an Irishman, did more harm than good, then they were off again, pivoting awkwardly on one foot.

Somehow, order emerged out of the chaos. As a unit they rushed up to and collected around Fargo.

Breathlessly, Blinky asked, "What do you want us to do? Fight from the outcrop?"

"No," Fargo began. "I'll take the women inside the outcrop while you men put the wagons in a defensive circle." Again he glanced at the riders, then added, "You better get a move on. They'll be on us before you can say scat."

Fargo motioned for the women to run to the outcrop, then headed that way. At the pond he told them, "Stay here and do not show yourselves. Charleen, I'm leaving you in charge. See that everyone obeys my orders."

"Why don't you and your guns stay here and protect us?" Charleen asked, in a civil tone for once.

Fargo filled in the unstated part of her question: "And leave all that good Irish whiskey for the riders?" Without pause he gave the answer, "Because if those riders prove hostile, they might kill Blinky and the others. I'd rather fight from the wagons than here. I can't guard this entire outcrop from within it. They would kill me for sure. Then where would that leave you women? In one hell of a bad fix, I'd say. Do what I say, Charleen, and don't argue. Stay down and be quiet. I don't want to hear one scream." Before she could challenge him, Fargo spun and sprinted through the gap.

The wagons stood in a circle a goodly distance away from the outcrop. Fargo ran to the center of them and spoke loud enough for the Irishmen to hear. "I want you men to lay on the exposed, outer side of the kegs."

"Aw, shit," Blinky cried. "You're gonna get us killed for sure."

"No," Fargo shouted over their grumblings. "I'm playing the odds they will hesitate when they see you are unarmed. I'll drop at least five of them during that hesitation. I will, that is, if they draw down on you."

"Why wait for them to pull iron?" O'Malley wanted to know.

Fargo ignored the question. He didn't have time to explain his unwavering feelings toward a person not aiming a firearm or otherwise threatening him or a friend with intent to kill. He yelled, "Shut up, O'Malley! You and the others do what I said."

Reluctantly, the Irishmen climbed onto the heap.

Fargo stood between the tart and chuck wagon to watch the approaching horsemen. As they came closer, he saw one wore a war bonnet. "Crossed-Eyes?" he muttered. "How did the Ute get ahead of us?" Fargo shouted over his shoulder, "Relax, boys. It's only the Ute." Coming for a refill, he reckoned. He walked out away from the wagons and waited for the Ute chief and his band of warriors to arrive.

As the pack of warriors drew near, they broke and formed into a straight line, with Chief Crossed-Eyes in the middle. They halted about fifty yards in front of Fargo. After a long intimidating pause, Crossed-Eyes dipped his war staff directly at Fargo. Two keg-bearing warriors rode halfway toward the big man and dropped the two kegs. From the way the kegs bounced, Fargo knew they were empty. He watched the warriors return to their positions in the line.

Momentarily, the chief dismounted—rather clumsily, Fargo thought. He watched Crossed-Eyes try three times to tie a white strip of cloth to the crook of the war staff. Failing on the third attempt, he flung the cloth to the ground, stomped on it, then missed completely when he tried to boot it.

Crossed-Eyes walked a crooked line coming to Fargo. Wobbly-kneed, he drifted left, then right, as though the act of walking were a labor for him. Fargo took pity on the old chief and met him halfway. The chief was in one of his left drifts and staggered past Fargo altogether. Fargo had to grab the man's arm to stop him.

The chief spun around. He seemed not to recognize Fargo. Fargo thought Crossed-Eyes didn't recognize anything or even know where he was. The man's breath reeked with Irish whiskey. Fargo winced from the smell of it. The chief made a face, shut both eyes tightly, then opened one. Fargo watched the dark iris make tiny circles, the red spider webs in the white around it oscillated wildly.

Crossed-Eyes slurred drunkenly, "Stand still. Stop darting in and out at me."

The old man's head roamed as though resting on a rubbery neck. The eagle feathers in his war bonnet were trying to take to wing. Fargo steadied the old man's head. It seemed to help. For a fleeting moment the eyeball quit rolling and the iris, normally aimed at the bridge of Crossed-Eyes nose, moved to dead center. "Aha," exclaimed the chief. "It's you, the paleface. Just the man I want to see."

"What about?"

"I'm in a trading mood, white man."

"What's there to trade, old man?"

"Whiskey or your scalp. I'm serious this time."

The old man squinted past Fargo. "Paleface, make those ugly buzzards stop staring at me.

Fargo glanced behind. The females had scaled the rocks. They hung by their fingertips. Only their ashen faces showed above the rocks. Fargo shouted, "I thought I told you women to stay down and be quiet."

Grace yelled back, "Aw, Fargo, darling, we—"

Maureen interrupted, "He isn't your darling, Grace Hatfield, Skye's *my* darling. Isn't that right, Skye, darling?"

There was only one fast way for Fargo to bring a halt to this nonsense. He fired one rifle shot over the women's heads. In unison their faces disappeared.

Crossed-Eyes grunted, "Good shot, paleface. You got all of 'em."

"Er, where were we, Chief?"

"Dickering. I said you people could keep your scalps in exchange for all that good Irish whiskey."

"Can't do it. Sorry."

"I'll kill you if you don't. My warriors will shoot so many arrows into those stupid Irishmen's bodies that they will look like porcupines. I'll prove it." Crossed-Eyes wagged his war staff.

Fargo watched a warrior dismount and step forward a few paces. The warrior placed an arrow on his bowstring. As he tried to aim the arrow at Fargo, both of the fellow's arms shook from the alcohol in them and under the tension of the bow. Finally, Fargo heard the bowstring twang. The arrow broke in two and so did the bowstring.

"So much for making porcupines out of us," Fargo muttered. In a stronger voice he said, "Chief, I can't stand here all day and palaver with you. I'm busy as hell, got more important things to do. I'll give you one keg, then you people be on your way."

Crossed-Eyes braced on his war staff. Squinting one eye, he said, "Horse pucky, white man. One measly keg? There's six or a dozen of us. I'll go for one keg apiece."

"One keg," Fargo repeated.

"Okay, then make it ten kegs."

"One," Fargo persisted.

The old man screwed up his face in a pained expression. "Have it your way. Twelve kegs."

"Two kegs, Chief. That's the best I can do. Take it or leave it."

Crossed-Eyes commenced a war dance. He whooped and hollered for a minute or so, then fell into Fargo's arms. He brought Fargo's chiseled face into focus and said, "Thanks, pardner. Make it fourteen kegs and I promise we won't bother you again."

Fargo forced a grimace. "Three kegs, or I'll scalp you here and now."

The old man broke a victorious smile. "You got a deal."

Fargo turned and yelled to the Irishmen, "Bring three kegs, boys."

They chorused, "Aw, shit! He's done it again."

Fargo turned back to Crossed-Eyes. "How did you get ahead of the wagons?"

Crossed Eyes pointed his war staff at the mountains in the east. "Shortcut. An old Indian trail."

"Wide enough for a wagon?"

"Do fish fuck in water?"

And that answered that. Now Fargo knew how the rogues and Germans got to the canyons. He posed another question to the old man. "What can I expect in front of me?"

The old chief's expression became serious. He stepped close to Fargo and whispered in a conspiratorial tone, "Beware while in the fog. Oden is there."

Fargo glanced toward Mean Canyon. "Fog? Oden?" he muttered.

Before Crossed-Eyes could explain, the Irishmen arrived with the kegs.

"Where you want 'em, boss?" Gotcheye asked.

"Anywhere. Then get in your driver's seats. I'll fetch the women. I want to be in Mean Canyon's opening before the storm strikes."

Fools Gold gestured toward the sky. "Storm? What storm? There's not a cloud in the sky."

"Nor will there be any," Crossed-Eyes mumbled.

Fargo didn't have time for Gotcheye's foolishness or Crossed-Eyes' riddles. He saddled and made the Ovaro ready for the trail, then went to the pond.

All the women had their backs flattened against the rocks. Wide-eyed, they stared at him. Charleen snapped, "You big idiot, you could have shot one of us."

"Thought about doing just that," Fargo began. "The only thing that stopped me was not being able to tell you twins apart. Now, get your butts in the wagon before I change my mind."

Grace interpreted to the tarts. They hurried to obey. Fargo chased Grace and the twins through the gap. The Ute had formed a tight circle around their chief. Like spokes on a wagon wheel, each held a tin cup out for Crossed-Eyes to fill from a keg.

Mounting up, Fargo told Fools Gold O'Rourke to take the lead position and Wee Willie to bring up the rear. He had Grace tell Can Can to put the tart wagon in front of the chuck wagon. O'Malley, Gotcheye, and Blinky followed in Fools Gold's ruts. He stationed the twins and their jenny between the chuck wagon and the tarts' wagon because he didn't want to hear Charleen's bitching. Fargo rode alongside Fools Gold's wagon. He and Crossed-Eyes exchanged peace signs as the wagons started rolling.

Fools Gold remarked, "I guess you know they'll be back for more."

Fargo nodded. With four more canyons to go, in as many days, he saw no reason to believe the Ute would not try. So far they had emptied three kegs and were working off three more. The only reason he parted with the last three so easily was in hope the Ute would get blind-drunk enough to fall by the wayside and not be able to catch up with the wagons. He asked, "Fools Gold, when you Irishmen left Denver how many kegs did you have?"

Fargo watched the Irishman look at the sun for the answer. After much rolling of his eyeballs and ticking off the count on his fingers, Fools Gold replied, "We started out with thirty kegs in each wagon. How many does that come to? I can't figure so good in my noggin."

"That adds up to one hundred and twenty kegs."

"Less those you gave away," Fools Gold was quick to remind.

"How many people are at your mine?"

"Five. Six, counting Miss Precious."

"Twelve, counting the tarts," Fargo began. "Seventeen, counting you men."

"Damn, you are a fast counter. Wish I could do that. Er, uh . . ." Fools Gold paused to nod toward the rear. "Uh, how about her?"

"Her who?"

"You know. That woman. Whatcha gonna do with her?"

Fargo chuckled. "Eighteen, counting that woman. She stays till spring. You men will take her back to Denver when you make your spring run to fetch whiskey. Back to the kegs. The way I figure it, that translates to nineteen kegs per month for the six months of the winter season."

Fools Gold's expression was a study in concentration. His eyeballs rolled back. The tip of his tongue moved across his upper lip. A nervous tic pinched at the outer corner of his right eye. Finally, Fools Gold asked, "What's translate mean?"

Fargo shook his head. He told himself he had to stop using such words when talking with the Irishmen. He didn't explain. Instead, he told the Irishman what Fools Gold really wanted to know. "It means one keg for every person each month, with one keg left over."

Fools Gold's shoulders sagged. His expression became glum. He muttered, "That ain't enough whiskey. Not near enough."

Fargo couldn't believe his ears. Did the Irishmen bathe in whiskey? "Why not, O'Rourke?" he asked.

"You'll see," Fools Gold mumbled. He stared ahead, as though in a trance.

Nothing more was said until the sun lowered behind mountains in the west. Glancing at the peach-colored evening sky, Fargo suggested, "It doesn't appear we will have to buck a night storm in Mean Canyon. I'll ride ahead and scout for a place to stop for supper."

Evening shadows darkened Meadowlark Meadow by the time Fargo reached the mouth of Mean Canyon. He reined the Ovaro to a halt just inside the wide opening. Steep walls towered high on both sides of the canyon. While the interior of the canyon was black as a starless night, he could still make out the jagged crests of the walls, although barely. They, too, would be engulfed in darkness momentarily. Fargo had seen enough. "This is as good a place as any," he told his horse. He dismounted and sat on a boulder at the entrance. While waiting for the wagons, he watched a full moon slowly appear over the mountain-tops in the east. He reckoned by the time they had finished eating supper, the moon would be high enough to bathe the canyon in its light. Then the wagons would make good time.

Fargo heard the wagons approaching. He stood atop the boulder and cupped his hands to his mouth. He shouted to Fools Gold, "Keep coming, O'Rourke. Go far enough to make sure Wee Willie's chuck wagon clears the opening."

When Fools Gold's wagon rumbled past the boulder, Fargo jumped to the ground and watched the shadowy forms of the other wagons go by. When he saw the chuck wagon, he told Wee Willie to halt.

The other Irishmen sauntered to the rear and joined Fargo and Fools Gold. Fargo gave them time to stretch kinks from their backs and limbs, then told them to start rounding up firewood.

Gotcheye grumbled, "Shit, we have to do all the work."

"Gathering firewood is women's work." Blinky added.

"Yeah, Fargo, everyone knows that," O'Malley said.

Fargo barked, "I said git."

They didn't leave right off. After taking a few cautious paces, everyone halted and turned to face the dark canyon. Fargo knew they were afraid. Soothingly, he said, "Fellows, I'll be right here with my guns. If anything bad happens, you can count on me to come running. Now, go collect the wood."

They spread out in a straight line, facing the canyon wall opposite the shadowy one where the females ran to squat. Holding hands, they started inching forward.

Wee Willie started fumbling for cooking utensils.

Grace said, "Fargo, darling, these tarts are cold. They need clothing. What are you going to do about it?"

Grace's question, and the preamble to it, sounded more like a wife's than anything else. She brought Fargo a problem to solve, without suggesting an answer. Games, he told himself. Will they never end? He answered with a question of his own, "What do you have in mind, Grace?"

Without hesitation, she allowed, "The men's shirts will do. If we have to run around half-naked, they can to. Fair is fair. Make the men give up their shirts."

Wee Willie overheard her. He muttered, "I ain't parting with my shirt."

Fargo told Grace that when the men came back, he would take a vote. She interpreted his decision to the tarts.

Shortly, the Irishmen returned. Each carried a few pieces of dead tree limbs. Arranging the wood for the fire, Wee Willie told them, "Fargo's gonna make us give our shirts to the tarts."

"Like hell," O'Malley cried.

Grace butted in. "He's going to take a vote."

"Well, that's different," Gotcheye offered, and he sighed a sigh of relief. "Everybody knows a vote is fair."

Wee Willie struck a match, touched it to the tender among the dry firewood. As the flame blossomed and spread, the women came closer and turned their fannies to the fire. Fargo noticed gooseflesh on more than one rump. He waited for the fire to knock off the chill in the air, then called for the vote. "All in favor of not giving shirts to the women raise your hand."

Five male hands shot up. One of the twins elbowed the other. Both raised hands. Fargo said, "Seven vote no. Now, all in favor raise your hand."

Grace and the six tarts raised a hand. "Seven vote yes," Fargo said.

Grace looked at him. "Fargo, darling, how do you vote?" she asked.

"Yeah, Fargo, how do you vote?" Blinky asked.

Fargo knew he'd be damned either way he went.

Charleen made it easy for him when she said most bitterly, "He doesn't get to vote, because he called for it."

Fargo looked across the fire at her and grinned. "I vote in favor of," he said evenly.

"That's not fair," O'Malley complained.

"Take off those shirts," Fargo growled.

They saw he wasn't fooling. They reluctantly began removing and handing their shirts to the tarts. There weren't enough to go around. Déjà Vu was left out. The twins had dressed in their extra set of garments. For an instant Fargo considered making Charleen give her shirt to Déjà Vu. He decided arguing with her wasn't worth it. He went to his horse, came back, and handed his poncho to Déjà Vu.

Moonlight bathed the canyon by the time they finished eating Wee Willie's meal. Fargo saw the canyon was wide and relatively straight, the floor unusually smooth. He reckoned the wagons would make good time. He asked Blinky, "What's at the far end of Mean Canyon?"

"Emerald Meadow," Blinky replied, then mumbled, "If we get there."

Fargo's coffee had cooled. Dumping it on the fire, he said, "Don't start that shit, Blinky. I'm in no mood to hear your bellyaching about being attacked." Gesturing down the length of the canyon, he went on, "There's nothing to be afraid of. Do you see anyone lying in wait?"

"No," Blinky admitted, then he quickly added, "but that doesn't mean they aren't there."

"Who in the blazes are they?" Fargo asked, slightly peeved.

O'Malley answered, "You'll see."

Fargo grunted his displeasure with the Irishmen. Fargo gestured his hopelessness with them. He growled, "Get on your drivers' seats. Start rolling. And I don't want to hear another word from any of you about being afraid. Nothing is going to happen." Fargo swung up into his saddle.

Moments later the wagons started moving forward. The chill air became increasingly warmer and still the farther the wagons penetrated into Mean Canyon. Rounding a soft bend, Fargo heard Fools Gold gulp, and he saw why. Up ahead a blanket of ground fog covered the floor of the canyon. The top of the fog shone an eerie white in the bright moonlight. Fargo saw no problem regarding passage through it. The fog was so low that it would cover less than half a wagon wheel's diameter. He said, "Keep rolling, O'Rourke. We can make it."

"That's what you say," Fools Gold replied.

Fargo rode ahead and halted in the fog. Looking down, he saw it barely came to the Ovaro's knees. He waved for Fools Gold to proceed. When the wagon came abreast of him, the big man said, "I'll ride ahead and make sure there aren't any big rocks in your path."

"You won't find any. Rocks ain't the problem."

Glancing at him, Fargo shot back, "Then, pray tell, what is?"

"Get ready," O'Rourke answered in a near whisper. "You'll find out soon enough," he added nervously.

Angry with the cowardly Irishman, Fargo banked his fires and grunted as he rode ahead, then he slowed the stallion to walk about twenty feet in front of Fools Gold's wagon.

The fog became deeper. Fargo looked behind. The wagon wheels were still at their original depth while the top of the fog nearly touched the Ovaro's belly. Fargo realized he had entered a decline on the canyon floor. He proceeded onward. The decline bottomed out at saddle height. Fargo motioned for Fools Gold to come on.

After all the wagons had come down the gentle decline and gone a short distance in the new depth of the fog—it covered the tops of the wagons—Fargo heard a most mournful sound. It sounded as though someone was blowing a horn, an unusually long horn, for the low, foreboding tone seemed to come from faraway. It sent a chill down Fargo's spine.

Fools Gold shouted, "Oh, no. Not Oden. Save us, Fargo."

Oden? Fargo thought, then remembered Crossed-Eyes also had mentioned the word. At the time, Fargo had thought it a Ute word. Now it appeared that he was wrong, for there was movement just below the surface of the fog. He watched that movement swirl the fog in several places. The disturbances moved steadily toward the wagons.

Wheeling the pinto, Fargo shouted, "Who are they, Fools Gold?"

"Norwegians from the Other Side of the Mountain Mine," O'Rourke called back. "They're fierce devils, meaner than mean."

Fargo headed for the tart wagon. He and the Norwegians arrived at the same time. Their heads poked out of the fog all around the tart wagon. One of the shaggy-haired men—a big bruiser with cruel blue eyes—wore a helmet with a pair of curved animal horns on it.

The women stood and commenced screaming. Lustful Norsemen pressed over the wagon's sides and grabbed at the tarts. The twins were pulled from their saddles. Fargo went to their rescue first. He dismounted to take on the two men carrying the twins away. Fargo grabbed a twin from behind. A tug-o'-war ensued, wherein the twin lost her pants to Fargo. She had no bloomers on. Her ass shone in the moonlight. Fargo got in front of the man and powered a fist into his stomach. The fellow doubled over, gasped for air. Fargo yanked the twin off the man's shoulder and told her to stay below the fog, then chased down the other man.

As he neared him, Fargo heard new threats erupt at the tart wagon. Blue-blackbeard's strong voice growled, "If it's a fight ye bloody Norsemen want, then it's a fight ye will get. Come on, mates, the prize is pussy." His growls were joined by the achtungers ooompapaing their mouth-tuba sounds.

Fargo muttered, "Good," as he caught and confronted the other Norwegian. The fellow stood shoulder deep in the fog. He carried the twin draped over his left shoulder. He had pulled her pants off and now held her in place with one of his fingers crooked in her fiery patch. She squirmed to beat hell, screamed insistently while pounding her fists on the brute's back. Fargo hissed, "Put her down, else I'll knock your teeth out."

The brute reached behind, ripped the twin's shirt off her body, and flung it in Fargo's face. Temporarily blinded, Fargo didn't see the hard jab coming toward his mouth, but he felt it. Dazed, he covered his face with a forearm and began weaving and bobbing while clearing the purple flashes from his head. The fellow's second punch glanced off Fargo's right shoulder, but the next one slammed into his gut.

Fargo bent below the fog, grabbed and yanked the brute's ankles. The big bruiser fell backward and lost his fingerhold on the twin. Charleen cried, "Ow! You big-fingered son of a bitch, that hurt."

Fargo was astraddle him quick as a wink. He pounded the man's face until he was sure the brute was unconscious. Then he groped for Charleen under the fog. His groping hand found one of her breasts. She screamed, "Let go of my tit, you big bastard." Then she bit Fargo's forearm and kicked him in the balls. Fargo let go.

He stood and jerked her to her feet. In a pained tone of voice he said, "It's me, Charleen. Stop biting and kicking me." She slapped him. He turned her back to him and clamped an arm around her waist. Charleen started pinching his arm. That hurt. Fargo snarled, "Stop pinching me, woman. I'm trying to rescue you."

"In a pig's eye, you are," Charleen hollered. "You're out to rape me and blame it on that smelly brute."

Grunting, Fargo pushed her aside and strode toward the melee at the tart wagon. Norwegians, Germans, and pirates were pulverizing one another. All wanted the same thing: a woman, any woman.

The tarts and Grace stood on the wagon bed to watch the men brawl. Fargo saw the wagon as a lifeboat adrift in a fog-enshrouded sea, the men shoulder-deep, treading in the water, fighting to climb aboard. He treaded his way through the combatants. He was pressing over the side when someone seized him from behind. Fargo glanced over his shoulder at the man. He was the one wearing the steel helmet.

Fargo heard Wee Willie cry, "Oh, no! Oden's got Fargo. We're doomed now."

Oden's hamlike fist closed Fargo's left eye and

jarred his brain. As he fell backward and before being swallowed up in the dense fog, Oden's pistonlike punches struck two more times: one in Fargo's chest, the second upside his head. Fargo groaned. His mind became as foggy as the ground on which he lay. He heard Oden stomping all around him. Oden's feet found Fargo's crotch. Suddenly, everything inside Fargo's skull turned black.

His sense of feel signaled his return to consciousness. A jackhammer was on the loose inside his skull. It was followed by his sense of hearing. He heard a weird mixture of ringing and buzzing. Smell returned next. Wood. His nose was pressed to wood. He tried opening his eyes. The right eyelid cracked open. Barely. He saw bare feet. Groaning, Fargo rolled onto his back.

The tarts, twins, Grace, and the Irishmen swirled around him. He closed the eye. Through the ringing and buzzing he heard Grace ask, "Fargo, darling, are you all right? Can you hear me, honey?"

It seemed to him as though she spoke from faraway. He opened the eye and brought her into focus, mumbling, "I'm okay. Just let me lie here to die. There is a loose cannon bouncing around in my brain. Shit, I hurt all over. What happened? Where did everyone go?" He tried to sit, but found he could not.

Maureen sat and cradled his head on her lap. She started the explanation. "Skye, darling, you're the bravest man I've ever known."

Brave? He didn't think so. The Trailsman got knocked out.

Maureen continued, "And the cleverest."

Clever? He wondered what he did that would permit her to say such a thing?

Grace picked up on the explanation. "You shouted to Wee Willie from below the fog."

"I did? Er, what did I say?"

"You told him to get your rifle off your horse."

Fargo cut his eye to Wee Willie. The Irishman smiled and held the Sharps out. He said, "I had me some fun, even though I was scared shitless and shaking all over. Anyhow, I waded through that fog to your horse and got the rifle. Now that I had it, I didn't know exactly what I was supposed to do. I—"

"You're rambling, Wee Willie," Fargo interrupted. "Get on with it."

Maureen replied, "I saw him get your rifle. Wee Willie dropped down in the fog and started shooting."

Wee Willie said, "I aimed straight up so's I wouldn't hit anybody."

Grace said, "When that rifle roared the first time, those men stopped slugging one another. They got real quiet and started looking around to see who got hit and who fired the bullet. Then, when Wee Willie fired again, all of them ducked below the surface of the fog. The tarts and I watched the fog swirl, so we knew the men were moving away from our wagon. The rifle roared again. This time those men picked up speed. When it roared a fourth time, they stood and started running full-speed. They were out of sight when Wee Willie fired again."

"How long was I out?" Fargo asked.

"Long enough for us to get through the fog," O'Malley answered.

Then Charleen said cuttingly, as only she could do, "Mr. Fargo, you are a big coward. I don't believe you're either brave or clever like my sister said. You were hired to protect us, and you did not. Look at me. I lost all my clothes. So did all the other women. Those men mauled us. And you just stood there and watched. You sorry bastard, you didn't lift a finger to help. What have you to say about that?"

The only thing Fargo could think of was "I didn't lift a finger because his was in the way."

9

The wagons rolled out of the far end of Mean Canyon at daybreak the next day. Spacious, lush green, and beautiful, Emerald Meadow stretched before them. Fargo vaguely saw it, though; dog-tired, he closed his eyes.

A high-pitched, grating noise, as though a child was scraping fingernails on a chalkboard, snapped them open. Partway. Enough so that out the corner of his eye he saw the tart wagon pass by. The racket came from the right front wheel.

Grace shouted, "Fargo, darling, you're fixing to fall out of your saddle."

As she sounded the warning, he started leaning to the right. The Ovaro halted.

Maureen rode up alongside the stallion and pushed Fargo erect. He slowly, with great effort, turned his head to face her. When she spoke, her voice sounded to him as though it came from the far end of a long tunnel, hollow and faint: "Skye, darling, are you all right? Why don't we stop and rest?"

He looked at her through blurred vision. Fargo saw them tumbling through space together. The stars and constellations swirled topsy-turvy. They collided with a planet. The crash didn't hurt. It felt soft and strangely cool on his face. Then darkness came.

Fargo awakened slowly. He lay flat on his back inside his bedroll, staring at a midafternoon sun.

When he moved, unbridled pain shot through his body from his toenails to the tips of the hairs on his head. When he yawned, every muscle in his chiseled-face ached. He hurt all over. Oh, God, how he hurt. His confused brain recalled his last conscious thought: the collision with the planet. Why am I not dead? he wondered. Maybe I am! Fargo extended a hand outside the bedroll and felt the coolness and texture of grass. Forcing himself to ignore the pain, he turned his head and saw mountains. Frowning—it hurt, too—he mumbled, "Where am I?" and that also hurt. Fargo turned his head to face the other way. Now it all came back to him. He wasn't on another planet. If he was, then the wagons, Irishmen, and women were with him. The wagons were parked end to end a short distance away, the people gathered around a fire next to the chuck wagon.

He didn't think the hurting he felt in the lower part of his belly was caused by last night's fog-bound fight with Oden Norgaard. It probably meant his bladder needed emptying. Fargo pulled the bedroll open. Somebody had undressed him. He propped on one elbow and looked for his clothes. They were neatly folded on the grass at the head of the bedroll. His holstered Colt and sheathed stiletto lay on top of the clothing. He didn't see the Ovaro. He whistled to him. The stallion trotted from behind the chuck wagon and came to Fargo. He saw the pinto had also been "undressed." With much excruciating pain—Fargo told himself he simply had to stop brawling—he swung onto the stallion's bareback and headed for a grove of aspen nearby.

He braced on an aspen while he pissed on its trunk. Turning, he saw Grace Hatfield had come to his bedding. He watched her roll and tie it, then sit and look toward the grove. Fargo stretched some of the soreness from his body, then started doing pushups and sit-ups to loosen the rest. Dancing around the tree, he threw a few punches. Satisfied that everything worked okay, he got on his horse and rode back.

Grace greeted him cheerily. "Fargo, darling, I was so worried about you. Get off that pretty horse and hug me close."

He looked at her nakedness, then his. "No, Grace. I don't feel like wrestling with you today. I'm too sore. I might not recover for several days."

"Who said anything about wrestling? I asked for a hug."

He slid her a wry glance. "Start handing up my clothes. The underwear first. Then you put on my shirt. It's the last one I have, so don't lose it."

Handing him the undergarment, her nipples brushed his right thigh. Their eyes met. Holding the eye contact, she pursed her lips provocatively, then kissed his thigh where her nipples had rubbed. Fargo allowed her that tad of enjoyment before pulling on his underdrawers. "My socks next," he said.

She tossed the socks to him. Pouting, she said, "You don't love me anymore."

Fargo pulled on his socks. "I said you can wear my shirt. Put it on."

"No. I don't want it. I'll go naked like the other females."

"Suit yourself, Grace." He slid off the Ovaro and picked up his shirt. Donning it, he asked, "Has Chief Crossed-Eyes showed up this morning?"

"No. What makes you believe he would?" A hint of concern crossed her face. "I'm afraid of Indians."

Strapping on the calf sheath, he allowed, "The Utes will be along because they want some more whiskey."

"My God, Fargo, you gave them three kegs just yesterday."

He nodded. He started one foot in the Levi's,

paused, and looked at her. "If I give you my Levi's, will you wear them?"

She shook her head.

He finished getting into the Levi's. Buckling up, Fargo's wild-creature hearing detected the soft sounds of slow-walking horses. As he pulled on his boots, he glanced toward the mouth of Mean Canyon. While he did not see the horses, he knew their sounds came from within the canyon. Nodding toward it, he said, "Crossed-Eyes will appear most any minute now."

Surprised, Grace looked that way. "I don't see him. You're just trying to scare me."

Fargo swung his gun belt around his waist and buckled it. "They are behind the last bend, coming toward us." He unhurriedly put on his neckerchief as he continued to gaze at the bend.

Grace repeated, "I don't see anything. Fargo, darling, you're imagining things. You sure you aren't still affected by the beating you took last night?"

He put on his hat, picked up his bedroll, and headed for the chuck wagon. At the fire he suggested that the women get in the tart wagon and sit.

Grace said, "He is hearing things." She shook her head sorrowfully, as one might do when in the presence of the village idiot.

Fargo filled a tin cup with Wee Willie's coffee.

The Irishmen looked toward the canyon. Gotcheye cast the big man a quick glance and asked, "You want us to put the wagons in a circle?"

"Not necessary," Fargo muttered sardonically. He sipped from the steaming brew, then explained, "The Utes are too drunk to fight. Crossed-Eyes will hound us till he gets some whiskey. I don't want or need that annoyance. So, you men might as well go ahead and get a few kegs ready for them."

O'Malley balked. "They ain't getting no more of

our whiskey. Not one keg. Ain't that right, boys? Huh, Fools Gold?"

Fools Gold mumbled his agreement. The others nodded theirs.

Fargo gestured toward the opening of Mean Canyon. "Here they come."

Everyone looked. The Utes had cleared the bend. Even at this distance they could see the Utes were stoned. All of them hugged their pony's necks. Two fell to the ground, staggered to their feet, and after great difficulty managed to get astride again.

O'Malley emphatically claimed, "Them Utes don't look in no condition to put up a fight. Anyhow, if they do," he snorted, "we can handle them. Right, boys?"

Fargo decided to let the Irishmen have it their way, if for no other reason than to teach them a painful lesson. He said, "Okay, you guys take care of them. I'll sit by the fire, drink coffee, and watch."

Charleen snapped, "You big coward."

He threw her a glance that might have said, "Woman, get off my back," then said, "Honey, you best get in the wagon. Take the other women with you."

"Don't boss me around, you big bastard." Charleen's eyes flared. She tossed her head, raised her chin, straightened her shoulders. Hands on hips, she hissed, "And don't call me honey. I loathe you. Oh, how I loathe you."

She had pushed him one notch too far. Grim-jawed, he stared into her eyes as he slowly rose out of the squat and poured the remainder of his coffee onto the fire. He dropped the tin cup and brushed his hands.

Maureen sensed what he was about to do. She cried, "No, Fargo. Please don't." Wringing her hands, Maureen glanced at her twin. "Charleen, I beg you to say you're sorry. Please, Charleen."

"Sorry for what?" Charleen spat. "I'm not afraid of your precious Skye Fargo."

Fargo's left hand shot around Charleen's waist. Taking her down with him, he sat with his legs spread, then turned her facedown and laid her across them. Then he started spanking her.

Charleen tried to wriggle free. She screamed, "Ow! Stop, stop. You lousy . . . Ow! You're hurting me, you big bully."

The Irishmen cringed as Fargo continued to put a blush on Charleen's rump. Maureen flinched on every slap. Grace moaned as she watched. The tarts headed for their wagon.

After a whack, Fargo paused to ask, "I'll quit if you promise not to bitch at me anymore."

"Yes, yes," Charleen cried. "Oh, my God, my butt is on fire. I'll promise anything, if you will only stop spanking. Anything, Mr. Fargo. Oh, God, that hurt. Please, please, don't spank me anymore."

He took away his restraining hand on her shoulder. Charleen lay there whimpering until Fargo told her she could get up. She rose onto her hands and knees. When she looked at him, he saw her eyes were filled with tears. She fell against him, clutched his powerful shoulders, and began to sob. Fargo cradled the shapely redhead in his arms and carried her to the wagon. Maureen and Grace followed. Fargo lifted her over the side and sat her on the floor.

Huddled together, the Irishmen watched the Utes approach. Fargo retrieved his cup. He sat and filled it, then listened to them argue about what to do. O'Malley was for taking them head on. He claimed the Ute were so drunk that they wouldn't know what hit them. Gotcheye favored leaving them tied up for the buzzards to feed on. Blinky wanted to break every bone in their bodies, and Fools Gold argued for taking their scalps. A consensus was reached when one of the warriors fell off his pony.

"See," O'Malley began excitedly, "what did I tell you? They're so drunk that they can't even ride."

As a unit, the Irishmen hitched up their pants and took one step forward. Sipping his brew, Fargo saw why the sudden halt. The warrior had his bow positioned to let an arrow fly. Unsteady on his feet, there was no telling where the arrow might go. As the warrior fell backward, he released the bowstring. Fargo and the Irishmen watched the arrow arch overhead and plunge into a keg on O'Malley's wagon. The keg immediately started to leak good Irish whiskey.

"You sorry, rotten bastard," O'Malley protested, loud enough to be heard all over Emerald Meadow.

The warrior stood. Fargo watched him pull another arrow from his quiver. Fools Gold grasped what was on his and the other Irishmen's minds, "Begorra, they are going to bloody well kill us."

The Irishmen ran to the other side of the chuck wagon. Fargo watched the arrow come down dangerously close to the tart wagon. When the archer got a third arrow ready to shoot, Fargo drew his Colt and shot off the high tip end of the bow. Shaking his head, he stood and holstered the Colt, then walked out a ways to meet the Ute.

The Indians were a motley lot, Chief Crossed-Eyes the motliest. From ten yards away Fargo could smell the invisible cloud of whiskey that enshrouded them. Crossed-Eyes tried a hand signal to halt them. But the half-assed gesture didn't work. The drunken warriors kept right on going toward the wagons. One nearly bumped into Fargo. He had to step aside and let the rider pass. When they got to the wagons, they rode between them and kept going. Fargo watched the Irishmen dive under the chuck wagon and crawl to the safe side.

Crossed-Eyes had halted his pony about eight yards in front of Fargo. Upon dismounting, the chief's left foot somehow snagged the reins. He fell awkwardly and landed facefirst on the ground, the foot still tangled in the reins. Eight strides put Fargo to Crossed-Eyes.

The chief twisted and looked at him. He broke a sheepish grin that didn't work out, then thick-tongued slurred, "Howdy, paleface."

Fargo got Crossed-Eyes' foot untangled. The Ute chief slumped to the ground and lay there blinking at the big man. Fargo squatted and said, "Chief, it isn't nice to terrorize these Irishmen. I want you to stop doing it."

Crossed-Eyes smacked his lips. Making a face, he said, "The inside of my mouth tastes like buffalo shit. I need a drink real bad, paleface."

Fargo pulled him up into a sitting position. Adjusting the chief's war bonnet, Fargo said, "If I give you one, will you go away and never bother us again?"

"You bet, paleface. Hurry."

Fargo ambled to O'Malley's wagon and got the leaking keg. On his way back to the chief, O'Malley called out to him, "Fargo, what do you think you're doing, giving our whiskey away?"

Fargo looked over his shoulder at Trevor. He noticed the warriors had turned around and were riding back to the wagons. Fargo shouted, "You boys better get ready for a fight. The Ute smell whiskey."

He squatted and handed Crossed-Eyes the keg. The chief pulled out the arrow, then put his mouth to the hole, reclined, and began sucking. Fargo let him go at it a long moment before taking the keg away. Crossed-Eyes instantly became panic stricken. His expression registered shock as he growled, "Paleface, you fool, who do you think you're toying with? Put that hole back where it was. Otherwise, I'll have to kill you."

Shaking his head, Fargo replied, "Only if you agree to get out of my hair. I still have three canyons to go, and I don't want to see you again."

Crossed-Eyes grabbed the keg. Fargo wrenched it from his grasp. Crossed-Eyes body fell limp. Not so with his soused mind. He said, "Paleface, what say we make a trade?"

Fargo chuckled. "Chief, you're in no condition to trade. But go ahead and try. I'm a tad curious to hear the what for."

"Whiskey for information." Crossed-Eyes reached for the keg.

Jerking the keg away, Fargo asked, "Oh, what information?"

"A secret." Crossed-Eyes focused on the hole, licked his lips in anticipation.

"What secret?"

"A twenty-keg secret."

Fargo sensed the chief indeed knew vital information. Just what, he didn't know. So Fargo probed for it. "No secret is worth twenty kegs of good Irish whiskey."

"This one is," Crossed-Eyes retaliated seriously.

Fargo suspected it had something to do with what lay ahead. He said, "Four kegs, Chief. That's all it's worth to me. I'll give you this keg and three more having no holes in them."

"Aw, shit," lamented Crossed-Eyes. "Can't you make it six kegs?"

"Four."

"Damn, paleface, you're a tough trader."

"Deal?"

Reluctantly, the chief agreed. "You won't back out?" the chief asked, a hint of fear in his voice.

"I keep my word, Crossed-Eyes. What's the secret?"

Flat on his back the old chief gestured toward the canyon beyond Emerald Meadow. "There is a secret cut in yon canyon. Watch for four blue spruce that stand alone next to the left wall. One is dead. Got struck by lightning. The cut is behind the dead tree."

Fargo felt as though the old man had just tricked him out of four kegs of whiskey. The knowledge of a cut through the canyon wall wasn't worth that many, he told himself. Shaking his head, Fargo looked thoughtfully at Crossed-Eyes.

Pain flashed across the old man's face as he whined, "You ain't gonna cheat me, are you, paleface? You can't trust a white man to keep a treaty. They'll break it every time. Damn, just my luck."

"I said I keep my word," Fargo reminded. "But what is so all-fired important about a passage through the wall? Is it wide enough for the wagons? Are you telling me there is a shortcut to Blood Gorge?"

"We take it all the time. Not wide enough for a wagon, though."

The old codger had indeed suckered him out of the whiskey. "Hunh!" Fargo snorted, his eyes all of a sudden more than miffed.

Crossed-Eyes continued, "So do those bad-assed miners."

Fargo raised his brows. Now, that is worth four kegs, he thought. Handing over the keg, Fargo went fishing. "Tell me more, Chief."

Shaky hands clutched the keg. The old chief raised it above his wrinkled face and removed his thumb from the bung hole the arrow had made. He caught the amber stream in his mouth and began gulping. Finally, he put his thumb over the hole and licked his lips.

"Well? I'm waiting, Chief."

"Don't rush me, paleface. Gotta catch my breath, you know. Where was I?"

"The miners."

"The rascals will be hunkered down behind that

burned tree, lying in wait for you to come by. Look for the dead tree."

"Er, uh, which miners?"

Genuine surprise formed on Crossed-Eye's face. His brows pinched as he squinted one eye and said, "Why, them Chinamen from the Ding Hao mine, of course."

Fargo's eyes kicked up. Frowning, he looked across the meadow at the near end of the distant canyon. "Chinese miners?" he muttered.

"Yep." The chief caught another mouthful of whiskey, then added, "They got a big gong. Real big. You'll hear the damn thing. They beat it real slow. Makes my blood run cold every time I hear it. Them Chinamen, they don't fight fair, either. Always leaping and kicking, yelling 'aahyee!' or something like that." Crossed-Eyes formed his lips around the hole and nursed on it.

Fargo stood and looked at the chuck wagon. The Utes had dismounted. Those not sprawled on the ground were attempting to war-dance around the fire. Fargo ambled over to them.

Rivers of nervous sweat poured off Blinky's head. He hugged Gotcheye, who shook like a quaking aspen leaf. Fools Gold clutched O'Malley tighter than Crossed-Eyes did the keg. Both gulped continuously. The swooping, war-whooping Utes brandished knives and tomahawks. Most appeared too dull to cut butter.

Fargo shook his head, picked up a cup, poured himself a cup of coffee. After taking a sip, he looked at the cowardly Irishmen and said, "Okay, boys, off-load three kegs."

The war dance instantly ceased. The dancers chorused an off-key cheer. O'Malley gagged, "Three?" You gave them three kegs?"

"No, I gave them four." Fargo nodded toward Chicf Crossed-Eyes. Fargo held up three-fingers to a big warrior, then gestured toward the nearest whiskey wagon.

The warrior looked at the Irishmen, as though asking for their permission. The Irishmen obviously took his stare as a prelude to him claiming their scalps. O'Malley was the first to capitulate. He nodded most vigorously. The other four were quick to follow his lead.

Smiling, the warrior sheathed his scalping knife, then embraced O'Malley. The Irishman's eyes rolled back and then he fainted. The warrior grunted, shrugged, and dropped O'Malley to the ground. Then he motioned for his companions to follow him to the whiskey wagon.

When the Utes staggered away, Fools Gold said in a trembly voice, "Whew! That was a close call."

Blinky and Gotcheye echoed his comment.

While he watched the Utes to make sure they took only three kegs, Fargo queried the Irishmen about the next canyon. "What do you men call the canyon we are coming to?"

"Big Windy," Wee Willie answered.

"That's because it's big and windy," Fools Gold added.

Gotcheye explained the windy part. "That wind howls fierce as all get out through Big Windy. Never know which direction it will blow from. Sometimes it blows in our faces, other times on our backs. Now and then it blows crossways. One thing you can count on, though, it will be blowing."

To that Wee Willie added, "That howling wind shifts them dunes."

"Dunes?" Fargo repeated. "Uh, sand dunes?"

"Yessiree," Blinky verified. "The bottom of Big Windy is plumb covered with sand. A regular desert, if I say so myself, although I never saw a desert personally. Saw pictures of one, but never in person. We have a helluva hard time in getting the wagons through Big Windy."

Fargo conjured up visions of Chinese leaping over sand dunes from behind. He saw the wagons bogged in sand, easy prey for the fast-moving Chinese. He saw them kicking him off the Ovaro, going, "Aahyee!" or something like that. He scratched his chin.

Fools Gold told him about the big part. "Big Windy is the widest and longest of all the canyons. That's why we call it Big Windy. Cain't hardly see the walls. That's because of the sandstorms."

Fargo scanned the horizons in hope to see thunderheads building. But all he saw was clear sky. He lowered his gaze to the Utes. They sat in a circle on the ground near the whiskey wagon, passing the three kegs around. But he shook his head instead and said, "We're burning daylight, boys. Head 'em up and move out. Somebody bring O'Malley out of his faint.

As he started for his horse, Fargo glanced at the women seated in the tart wagon. He turned and caught the Irishmen before they got to their wagons. He told them to gather next to the tart wagon.

"What for?" O'Malley mumbled.

"Take off your pants, Trevor. All of you other boys do the same."

"Why?" Wee Willie whined.

"He's going to give our pants to the redskins," O'Malley began. "I just know he is. Fargo gives everything away. First our whiskey, then our shirts. Now he wants our pants. Well, not mine, he ain't."

Fargo squinted at O'Malley. That one squint was all it took for O'Malley to come out of his pants. The others were fast to follow suit. All stood in long johns. Fargo collected the garments and tossed them into the tart wagon, then he explained, "Grace, tell the tarts to put 'em on."

"There's not enough to go around," she said.

Fargo pulled his off and handed them to her.

"What about me and Charleen?" Maureen asked. "Don't we get any?"

Fargo didn't have a ready answer. But he thought of one. He went to the circle of Indians and found three who had passed out. Fargo came back with three buckskin aprons and three pair of moccasins. Passing by the back end of the wagon, he pitched them inside and muttered, "If they're good enough for Indians, they're good enough for you." He proceeded to the Ovaro and made him trail-ready.

Moments later the wagons passed the circle of Indians. Fargo watched as one staggered to his feet, fumbled with his bow and arrow, and finally got off a shot. The arrow twanged when its flint point stabbed into the driver's seat only inches away from O'Malley. The Irishman glanced at the vibrating shaft, then at the reeling warrior, and keeled over in another faint. Fargo shook his head.

The sun was half down on the horizon when a hot wind that carried sand greeted Fargo at the tight entrance to Big Windy. The Ovaro stood ankle-deep in fine-grain, reddish-white sand. Fargo pulled his neckerchief up to just below his eyes, then scanned the length and breadth of the canyon as far as the swirling sand permitted. Small dunes rippled a pattern that allowed Fargo to see a way through them. He had seen and conquered sandy terrain like this only once—in Death Valley over in Western Utah Territory. The mere thought of that ordeal triggered a shudder. He had found that weaving through the valleys of those dunes was faster and safer than riding a straight course over them.

Accordingly, he drew down on his painful Death Valley experience and halted Blinky, who drove the lead wagon. "Blinky, I'll ride ahead and show you the way. If I raise a hand, it means halt."

Blinky started blinking and stammered, "I—I'm scared shitless, Fargo."

Fargo believed him. He said, "Take it easy, Blinky. We will get through. I'll keep you in sight. Just follow me." Fargo nudged the stallion to proceed.

Soon the stars twinkled, the bright moon rose, and the hot wind began to howl. Immersed in the dunes, Fargo plunged through the sand blasting his and the stallion's face. Like a stormy sea, the wind knocked the crests off the dunes and made it near impossible for him to see Blinky's wagon. Knowing the little Irishman was concerned, Fargo dropped back a tad. Blinky gestured that he was all right.

Progress through the meandering valleys was slow. The swirling clouds of sand didn't make it any easier. Fargo rode atop a taller dune to scan for the dead spruce. Even at this elevated point the dense sand-clouds hid both walls of the wide canyon. Fargo reckoned if he couldn't see the tree, then the Chinese miners couldn't see the wagons, and the fierce, howling wind certainly absorbed all sounds made by the wagons. Satisfied that all was well, Fargo rode back down the dune and went to Blinky.

"How much farther before we get out of this mess, Blinky," he asked.

"We've gone 'bout halfway," Blinky shouted back. "It gets worse from here on."

That figures, Fargo mused to himself. He nodded and shouted, "Blinky, think you can stay in the troughs long enough for me to check on the tarts?"

"Sure. No problem."

Fargo dropped back. Passing the next wagon, he shouted, "You all right, Fools Gold?"

"Eating sand," Fool's Gold answered.

"Aren't we all?" Fargo replied.

At the third wagon Fargo swung around and rode alongside Can Can. She drove with her chin on her chest and her free hand protecting her bare bosom. He couldn't do anything about her bosom, but he could in regard to her bare face. He removed his neckerchief. Holding it out to her, he gestured for her to tie it around her head. Can Can quickly complied.

Fargo dropped back a tad to check on how the other females were faring. They sat in a group, huddled low behind the driver's seat. All had their knees drawn up to their chests, their arms wrapped around their shins, and their faces pressed to their kneecaps. Fargo decided they were all right. The twins' jenny, however, was in no way all right. As Fargo encouraged the pinto to quicken his pace, the jenny had a hee-hawing seizure that included bucking and kicking. The collection of pots and pans hanging on her clattered and clanged to beat hell. When combined with her continuous hee-haws, it made enough racket to wake the dead. Fargo dropped back and calmed the frightened old girl.

That's when he heard something mighty strange carried in the wind. Keenly alert now, he rushed to Blinky's wagon. Riding alongside him, he asked, "Blinky, are my ears playing tricks on me? Do you hear music in this wind?"

Blinky stiffened. His eyes got nearly as big as the scared jenny's. Blinky cried, "No, but, oh, shit, I know what it is." Nervous tics appeared at the outer corners of Blinky's rapidly batting eyes.

Fargo knew the terror-stricken man was in no condition to answer any further questions or even explain his remark. Fargo rode to get out in front of Blinky's team, where he could hear better.

And sure enough, he did hear music. A drum and fife accompanied by a bagpipe were playing "The Gary Owen." Standing in the stirrups, Fargo signaled for Blinky to halt. He wondered what on earth he had gotten himself into this time. Crossed-Eyes had said for him to listen for a slowly beating gong and to watch for leaping Chinamen.

Fargo watched a huge, fiery-red whiskered fellow blowing the bagpipe emerge from the cloud of sand. The man came over the top of the dune right in front of Fargo. He was followed by two others who played bagpipes also. Then came the drummer and three fife tooters.

"Crossed-Eyes, you lied to me," Fargo muttered under his breath.

As the seven definitely non-Chinese men came down the sandy slope to Fargo, the drum and fifes fell silent, the bagpipes gasped out the final notes of "The Gary Owen." The whiskered giant thrust out his right hand to Fargo, which he took. The man had a strong grip. Fargo reckoned him to be about ten years his senior. Flaming unruly red hair poked out all around the black-and-white-checkered topknotted tam cocked jauntily on the fellow's head. A bulbous nose and bushy eyebrows—also unruly—dominated his facial features. Piercing green eyes looked into Fargo's lake-blues. As he shook the hamlike hand, Fargo reckoned the man was friendly enough. As a matter of fact, all of them did. Weird, yes, but friendly and civil for a change.

Whiskers put a twinkle in his eyes when, in a whiskey voice, he asked, "Hoot, mon, what are you doing riding with these cowards from Blood Gorge?"

Fargo touched the Colt's handle to place emphasis on his answer. "Protecting their whiskey. What's your name? Mine's Skye Fargo. Some call me the Trailsman."

Whiskers laughed uproariously. When he laughed, the other six did, too. When he stopped, they also stopped. Whiskers said, "Some call me a big son of a

bitch. Some call me a big turd. Most call me dangerous. But, mon, nobody says I play bad music on me
darlin' bagpipe, which I call Highland fling. My name
is Dan McGrew."

"Well, Dan, what brings you out in this sand-
storm?" Fargo inquired, although he already knew the
answer.

"Whis—" Dan cut the word short. Fargo watched
his brows furrow, his head tilt upward, and his nostrils
flare, as he sniffed.

"What's wrong?" Fargo began. "What do you
smell?"

Dan squinted at him. "Pussy. A whole lot of
pussy."

From upwind? Fargo thought. In a howling sand-
storm? The man has to possess the world's best sniffer
to do that. Fargo scanned the faces of the men flank-
ing McGrew. All appeared mine-digging tough. But
McGrew was the boss. What Dan McGrew said, went.
So far Dan and his companions had not seen or heard
the women. Fargo was sure about that. He also knew
he would not be able to talk McGrew into turning
around and going back to wherever they came from.
And he wouldn't shoot unarmed men under any cir-
cumstance. Moreover, Fargo had brawled enough in
the last few days to last him a lifetime. Alone,
McGrew would be tough to handle. The other six
would, on command from Dan, most assuredly pulver-
ize him, then do with the women and whiskey what
they willed. Fargo didn't dare let them get one step
closer to the wagons. He drew his Colt and Sharps,
pointed the revolver at McGrew's massive chest, the
rifle at the drummer, and said evenly, "Scotchman,
do an about-face. March over that dune. I want to
hear music when you do." He thumbed back the
Colt's hammer.

Dan briefly studied the working end of the Colt's

barrel. When he shifted weight to the other foot, Fargo kept his aim centered on the giant's chest. Dan's eyes kicked up to Fargo's. Dan promised, "We will come again."

Fargo watched the big Scotsman turn and lead his men up the dune. They were quickly swallowed in the churning sand. Fargo tracked their retreat by listening to them play "The Gary Owen." He wondered if it was the only tune they knew. Satisfied they were moving away, he uncocked and holstered the Colt, returned the Sharps to its saddle case.

He rode to Blinky's wagon. Blinky was nowhere in sight. He found him cowering with the other Irishmen under the chuck wagon. Fargo dismounted and squatted to have a little chat with them. "You men can come out now. They have gone."

Gotcheye wasn't convinced. In a trembly voice he repeated McGrew's parting promise. "They'll be back."

The others nodded their agreement.

For the moment, Fargo ignored their concern about the Scots reappearing. He was more concerned about getting out of Big Windy. "First things first," Fargo began. "We have to leave Big Windy as fast as we can. Dan McGrew has one hell of a nose. From upwind he can smell a woman a mile away. So here's what we do. Wee Willie, you and Trevor get that sheet of canvas and cover it over and around the women. Blinky, you drive the tart wagon. I'll drive yours."

"Won't make any difference," O'Malley interrupted. "They will find us, anyhow. You'll see."

"Maybe they will and maybe they won't," Fargo replied. "We'll cross that dune when we come to it."

"Uh, what dune?" Fool's Gold wanted to know.

Fargo's shoulders sagged. Exasperated with himself for saying it, he sighed, then moved on to his next concern. "Now you are going to tell me what I can expect to find when we pass through the last two canyons. Wee Willie, you tell me."

"First, we have to cross Scorched Valley to get to Trouble Canyon. The good ol' boys from Alabama Barking Spider Mine always attack us in Trouble Canyon."

Fools Gold hurried to add, "They really stink." He pinched his nose for emphasis.

Wee Willie continued, "After Stench Canyon comes Snake Valley, then Deadly Canyon. That's where leaping and kicking Chinamen from Ding Hao mine attack. They take what whiskey the other miners didn't carry off."

Fargo asked, "And the Ute?"

"You can count on them being in Scorched Valley and Snake Valley," Wee Willie answered. "I don't know how they do it, drunk as they get, but they're always there."

Fargo nodded. Now he knew what he needed to know. He stood and told them, "Wee Willie, get the canvas. The rest of you men climb into your driver's seats." Having given them his marching orders, he led the black-and-white stallion to the front of Blinky's team and looped the reins loosely around the saddlehorn. Scratching the pinto's face, he said, "Boy, you lead and I'll follow. Take us out of here." Fargo had faith he would do just that.

The hot wind howled. Clouds of swirling sand diffused the bright moonlignt. The powerful stallion wove his way through the troughs of oceanlike monstrous waves. Skye Fargo, the Trailsman, figured out a plan should the miners reappear.

He grimaced at the thought of it.

10

The moon sunk below the horizon. Stars began to twinkle out. Skye Fargo watched dawn's early light filter through the blowing sand. He had halted twice and walked back to O'Malley's wagon and asked him how much farther. Both times the Irishman shook his head. Now, hours later, Fargo sensed the other end of Big Windy was near. An increase in the wind's strength led him to believe that it was so. The Trailsman knew about vortices. Although he couldn't see the walls of the canyon, he knew the space between them was narrowing. The open end of the canyon would be severely constricted, hence, the vortex. The hot wind blowing across Scorched Valley was like water. Both sought the path of least resistance. The wind built up at the constricted opening, then shot through it. Like water, the wind became its strongest as it gushed through the opening.

Through the blowing sand Fargo saw the stallion raise his head, his ears perk and swivel. The pinto had heard a new sound, one that didn't belong with the monotonous howl of the wind. Fargo watched the stallion's ears scan a ninety-degree swath in front of him, then point dead ahead. He had pinpointed the direction from where the sound came. Fargo focused all attention forward. He strained to hear the bagpipes, fifes, and drum, but heard only the screaming wind.

The stallion halted. Fargo reined to a halt behind

him. A monstrous dune had blocked the Ovaro's path. There were no troughs for him to follow. Fargo dropped from his seat. He plodded up to the wind-blown crest of the sand dune to find a way around it and out of this miserable canyon. Instead, he found miners gripping shovels. All of them stood looking up at him from the bottom of the dune they had obviously created.

Fargo had expected the Scots only. But he now saw he had been wrong in making that assumption. Also leaning on shovels were Blue-blackbeard and his rogue pirates, Ooompapa and his achtungers, and Oden Norgaard and his Norsemen.

Dan McGrew voiced what was on Fargo's mind: "Hoot, mon, 'tis the end of the line. There are more of us than your guns have bullets. We intend to have the whiskey and women."

Fargo knew a bad situation when he saw and heard one. Honor-bound to protect all and everything that stood behind him, he snarled, "Go back to your mines. Otherwise I will have to hurt you. Don't force me to do it."

When McGrew laughed, even the screaming wind could not absorb the other's laughter. McGrew stabbed his shovel in the sand and started up the slope. He waved the others forward.

Fargo came down to meet him. As he did, he modified his original plan. It's now or never, he told himself. Fargo shoved McGrew down the slope, then followed him to the bottom. Scanning the miner's surprised faces, he said, "Short of killing me—and I promise I'll kill at least five of you before that happens—there is only one way for me to give up the whiskey and women."

"Oho, me bucko, and what might that be?" Blue-blackbeard wanted to know. "Yer in no position to bargain."

"Let him speak his piece," a Norwegian shouted.

Coming to his feet, McGrew agreed. "And be quick aboot it, laddie."

Fargo cited his deal: "I'll fight the miner's four leaders one at a time. If I lose to any one of them, you take the whiskey and women. On the other hand, if I best them all in a fair fight, then you clear a path for the wagons and let us pass without giving us any more trouble."

McGrew smiled. He turned and asked the three leaders if they agreed to Fargo's terms. They nodded. McGrew asked Fargo who he wanted to challenge first. Fargo nodded toward Blue-blackbeard. The rogue handed his hat to one of his men and stepped forward. Fargo removed his gun belt and put it on the slope. The miners quickly formed into a circle around the combatants. The contest began.

Fargo touted his opponent into swinging and jabbing as hard and often as he could to make the man tire while conserving his own energy. Fargo waited for an opening to take out Blue-blackbeard with one punch. It came, but only after Blue-blackbeard drew blood first, a left jab that connected with Fargo's nose. Fargo caught him with a sledgehammer uppercut. The rogue catapulted backward, unconscious before he met the sand. Fargo drug the back of his left hand across his bloody nose and pointed with his right at Ooompapa. Rogues pulled their leader from the circle as the burly German stepped into it.

Firing up his tuba sound, Ooompapa tried to make short work of his adversary. He lunged and tackled Fargo around the waist. Going down, Fargo hit him twice upside the head. Neither blow fazed the big German, or shut down the tuba. He pulled Fargo to his feet, then drove a fist into his gut. Fargo doubled over, gasped for air. Ooompapa flung an uppercut that straightened up Fargo. Through blurred vision,

Fargo saw Ooompapa's huge right fist rushing to his face and ducked and grabbed Ooompapa's left ankle, then jerked. The burly fellow reeled and stumbled into a Norsemen's open arms. Dazed, Fargo backed into the crowd on the opposite side of the circle. Shaking his head to clear it, hands shoved him back into the arena.

Ooompapa charged like an enraged bull. Fargo nimbly sidestepped the onrushing human battering ram. He clasped both hands and hit the back of the German's big head as hard as he could. Ooompapa skidded facedown in the sand. He did not get up. Two of his men hauled him out of the circle.

Breathing hard, sweating profusely, Fargo checked his jaw to see if it was still in one piece, then wiggled a finger for Oden to come on. A sinister scowl flashed across Norgaard's hard face. He cracked his knuckles as he started moving around Fargo.

Fargo intended to get his payback here and now. His right foot lashed out. The boot's tip struck Oden's balls. Grabbing at the hurt spot between his legs, the Norwegian groaned loudly.

The spectators sucked in a breath, gasped, "Unfair! Low blow! Cheater! Cheater!"

Fargo backed away and gave the steel-helmeted man time to recover.

Oden nodded that he was ready to continue. He tried to grapple with Fargo. Fargo knocked his hands away and threw a left hook. Oden ducked. The blow glanced off his helmet. Oden slammed a fist upside Fargo's head. Fargo shook it off. Oden hit him again, this time in the chest. Fargo retaliated with three fast jabs to the face. Oden covered up, bent at the waist, and started weaving. Fargo's fists moved pistonlike until they pounded Oden's hands away from his face. Then Fargo uncorked a haymaker. Oden went down without so much as a grunt.

The behemoth Scot stepped over Oden's limp body to take on Fargo. Eyeing the big man, McGrew growled, "All you miners that are thirsty for the taste of Irish whiskey and pussy, crowd in closer. I'll finish him off."

The circle immediately tightened. McGrew's massive bulk loomed like an impregnable block of granite. Hands on hips, McGrew bent slightly and stuck out his chin, clearly inviting Fargo to take the first swing. He didn't flinch when Fargo reached out and positioned his jaw for the knockout blow. McGrew held the new angle while he watched Fargo's right fist cock.

Fargo threw his best Sunday punch. It slammed against granite. McGrew did not go down. He chuckled and rubbed his jaw. Fargo stared in disbelief at his skinned knuckles. Then sky rockets burst a spectacular rainbow of colors inside Fargo's skull.

He came to with his face bouncing on something soft and warm. He opened one eye and saw a breast. The nipple on it gouged just below the eye. He turned his aching head and saw bright sunlight on the wagon's bed. The nipple stabbed in his ear. He felt a pair of legs jostling on the backs of his. Fargo rolled over. As he did, her legs left his. He sat between them.

Grace Hatfield's arms snaked around his chest. She said, "Does your head still hurt? You have been groaning and holding it all morning."

McGrew sat Indian-fashion, with his back to the rear of the wagon. A twin sat on either side of him, the tarts lined the sideboards. Fargo noticed the Irishmen's pants had not been ripped off the tarts, and the wagon was passing over blackened land.

Grace tapped his left pectoral muscle. "Well, Fargo, darling, does it?" she asked again.

"Yes," he muttered.

McGrew explained, "Mon, you nigh broke my jaw. You're a tough mon, Fargo."

"Not tough enough, I see," Fargo began. He met each of the twins' gazes and said, "I'm sorry."

"For what, Skye, darling?" Maureen said.

"I failed you."

McGrew draped an arm over each of the twins' shoulders. "These two darlin' wee lassies told us you were honor-bound to protect them. We miners understand honor."

"Are you saying you didn't bother them?"

McGrew chuckled. "Mon, it's a game we play. The Irishmen go get the whiskey. Blue-blackbeard watches for them to come back from his position at Horror Canyon. Ooompapa watches from his at Worser Canyon, and so on. We see who can steal the whiskey first. Only we don't really take the kegs. We escort the wagons to Blood Gorge, then all of us get riproaring drunk and take turns on Miss Precious Goodbody."

Fargo nodded, although he thought it was an odd game.

McGrew continued, "This trip was different. The Irishman also brought back tarts. Mon, miners are forever in bad need of women. You know that. So we took them on the spot, or tried to. You fought hard to protect the lovelies and the Irishmen and whiskey. And you succeeded until we stopped you at the far end of Big Windy. We worked half the night piling up that sand."

Hugging him close, Grace said, "Now you know everything, Fargo, darling. Pleased?"

"Relieved is more like it," Fargo answered. "At least I now know I won't collect any more knots on my head."

McGrew corrected, "Mon, you still have two canyons to go. Bubba Jones and his men from the Alabama Barking Spider mine will be watching from the first, and Fa-ting and the boys from Ding Hao at the second. They're tough."

"Fa-ting?"

McGrew nodded. "Most Chinese can't say the 'r.' They drop it. Farting is what they are trying to say. Fa-ting farts a lot."

"Yeah, I know. I met him in Chinatown at Carson Valley, Western Utah Territory. A fat, jolly cook."

"Not anymore. He's skinny as a rail. Still jolly, though."

Squinting at Dan, Fargo wanted to make sure he heard right about him having to fight Bubba and Fa-ting. Fargo's hearing still buzzed, as though sand ran through the veins. "You telling me you people are going to stand off, say nothing, do nothing, not lift a finger, and let them attack the wagons? After all I've been through?"

McGrew nodded. "The game goes on. Hoot, mon, they deserve their chance. You don't know what it is like, waiting and watching. Normally, if they saw any miners riding with the Irishmen, that would mean they had already captured the kegs. They would come down through secret fissures in the walls and join the Irishmen, without harassing them."

Fargo frowned. "Secret fissures?"

"Hoot, mon, how did you think we got on the canyon floor? Jump? There are cracks in the walls big enough for a man to use. Except for Worser Canyon. Nary a single crack in those walls. But there are overhangs. The achtungers have to slide down ropes."

Crossed-Eyes hadn't lied after all, Fargo mused. He attributed the old man's drunkenness as the cause for his mistake in regard to the dead spruce. Simply put, Crossed-Eyes was two canyons ahead of himself. Fargo asked two questions: "Do the Irishmen know where the fissures are located? Do the Ute figure into the game?"

"Yes, to both questions. Because you were with the wagons, the Irishmen acted like cowards and let you handle things. The trick for them to perform is to get the whiskey through as many of the six canyons as they can, anyway they can. You got through the first three.

"We play for rewards and penalties. At their place, the Shamrock in Blood Gorge, the kegs are divided by seven. Each group of miners gets one-seventh share. The Irishmen are rewarded one-half the kegs due a group if they can get through their canyon. Blue-blackbeard is penalized half his share for letting the wagons through. So is Ooompapa and Oden. The Irishmen have never made it through all six canyons. The best they've ever done was four. Incidentally, just so you will know, Blue-blackbeard and his rogues aren't real pirates. His name is Peter Borland. He was born and raised on a Virginia farm. You saw his flint-lock pistols? They don't work. The rogues are from all over, like most of us."

"You haven't answered my second question," Fargo said thoughtfully.

"The Ute work the valleys and meadows between the canyons. Their role in the game is to slow down the wagons, then tell the next group of miners where the wagons are. Their reward is one keg every time they stop the Irishmen."

"Ye gods," Fargo cried. "I've given Chief Crossed-Eyes a total of ten kegs so far."

McGrew stiffened. "Ten kegs? Ten? Hoot, mon, have you lost your mind? At best he was due four."

"The old coot gulled me," Fargo admitted hollow-toned, more to himself than McGrew. At least he now knew why the Irishmen had kicked up a fuss. He promised himself that if the Ute appeared again he would penalize them for not playing fair. Crossed-

Eyes doesn't get another drop of drink, he told himself.

"You didn't know the rules," Grace said in Fargo's defense.

Fargo began a new query, even though he perceived McGrew's answer to it: "Back to Bubba and Fa-ting. Why will you allow them to try to capture the flag?"

"They don't know aboot these fine lassies. Your job is to protect them, if you can. At least these two who I have my arms around."

"I adore being wanted," Maureen allowed through a heavy sigh. "Men fighting for me, and all that."

Charleen snapped, "Maureen, you're as disgusting as Fargo. Have you forgotten?"

Fargo wondered what? He watched Maureen lean a tad so she could see her twin's eyes, then the two begin eye-talking. They're up to something, Fargo thought. Something bad. He closed his eyes, laid back against Grace's bosom, and quit trying to figure out what Charleen meant. The humdrum squeaks and groans of the wagon, and the steady rumble of its wheels, soon put Fargo to sleep.

An hour later O'Malley shouted, "There they are!" and jarred Fargo's eyes open. He sat and looked around. McGrew gestured for him to look forward. Fargo peered around Can Can's derriere and saw dark thunderheads moving in from the west. At first he reckoned the ominous clouds had prompted O'Malley's shout, and lowered his gaze to see how far the wagons were from Trouble Canyon. The Utes were strung out in a long line, moving across the burned stubble in the valley on a course to intercept the wagons. Chief Crossed-Eyes rode the lead pony. Fargo twisted toward McGrew and asked, "How does he do it? We leave them blind-drunk, sitting on the ground, and the next thing I see they are well ahead of the wagons."

"Mon, they take the high road. It's straight and fast."

"There's a road up there? Wide enough for the wagons?"

McGrew nodded. "The road changes into a footpath aboot midway above Trouble Canyon. I know what you're thinking—why take the miserable canyons when there is a perfectly good road above them? That right?"

Fargo nodded.

McGrew made it brief. "Makes the game more interesting."

Fargo shook his head. For a moment he considered telling the twins to mount up and the three of them leave the miners and Irishmen to play their stupid game. But Charleen changed that when she said, "Mr. Fargo, my sister and I have decided to winter at Blood Gorge. We haven't done one painting since we met you. Winter scenes of Blood Gorge would be beautiful. Get us safely to Blood Gorge and your job is done. And, yes, you can keep the money."

So, Fargo thought, that's what all the eye-talk was about. He chuckled "But you never paid me," and then whistled for the Ovaro.

As the stallion trotted up alongside the tart wagon, McGrew raised his bushy eyebrows and commented, "Damn smart horse you have, mon. Want to sell or trade him?"

Stepping from the wagon into his saddle, Fargo said, "Thank you, but he's not for sale or trade."

Fargo rode up alongside Blinky's wagon. Blueblackbeard sat beside the Irishman. About a halfdozen miners rode with the kegs. The other miners did likewise in the other wagons. Most drowsed. Fargo waited and watched the Ute make their intercept.

Crossed-Eyes, like all the warriors, was having difficulty staying on his pony. He would lean way over to one side until Fargo thought the man would surely fall, then catch and hold, only to nearly roll off the other side. By the time he got to Fargo and the pony halted of its own accord, the old man had gotten turned completely around and collapsed facedown on the pony's rump. Crossed-Eyes' arms hung down either side of the pony's rump, his old wrinkled face buried in its tail.

Fargo gently pulled him into a sitting position. While the chief's head lolled, Fargo saw his eyes were no longer crossed, but they were severely bloodshot. The old man swung his head around and up. Through a crooked, silly grin, he said, "Aha! I gotcha now, paleface. Whiskey or death? You choose."

"How many kegs this time, Chief?"

"Fifty. Make it snappy or I'll kill you on the spot."

Fargo grabbed the pony's hackamore and led the horse to stand next to the tart wagon. He held the chief's head steady and turned it to face Grace Hatfield, then asked, "What do you see, Chief?"

His answer came quick. "I see an ugly white woman."

"I'm giving her to you instead of the whiskey."

"No, you're not," Crossed-Eyes shouted. "I don't want an ugly woman."

"Yes, you do."

"No, I don't." The old man started bawling. Real tears rippled down his wrinkled cheeks. The eagle feathers in his war bonnet shook. The white strip of cloth tied to his middle finger shook. He sobbed so hard he shook all over. Fargo heard him whimper most pitifully, "I need a drink real bad."

Fargo looked at McGrew, who made a helpless gesture. There was nothing for Fargo to do but put the drunken man in the wagon. Grace had tears of pity in her Christian eyes as she helped Fargo get him in it. In short order he had all the Ute draped over kegs.

Then he strode to the Ovaro, mounted up, and shouted, "Roll 'em, you Irishmen! I want to be in Trouble Canyon when the storm strikes." Skye Fargo intended to take them good ol' boys head-on. "It's the only fast way to get away from the twins," he muttered under his breath.

The dark clouds loomed dangerously close dead ahead. Lightning walked about in them. A chilly breeze blew in advance of the clouds. A low rumble of thunder droned out of the canyon, rolled across Scorched Valley. Rain was imminent. As the clouds blotted out the rapidly lowering sun, Fargo stared at the wide opening of Trouble Canyon only moments away.

As he entered the canyon, the miners and Ute abandoned the wagons, a monstrous lightning bolt peeled a Douglas fir nearby, and a gargantuan thunderclap ushered in a torrential downpour.

McGrew found Fargo and said, "Laddie, we're going now and taking the Ute with us. We'll follow you on yon ridge." He pointed to the left wall, then added a warning, "Bubba Jones doesn't fight fair. We will be watching." He threw Fargo a salute, fired up his bagpipe, and sauntered away.

Fargo rode through the deluge to Blinky's wagon. He shouted to the Irishman, "How long is this canyon, Blinky?"

"Short. About two miles."

"Where is the crack the good ol' boys come through?"

"About midway. I'll point to it when we draw near."

"Which side?"

"Left wall."

"Don't stop for anything."

"Don't worry. I won't."

Fargo nudged the Ovaro's flanks. He rode to and

followed the contour of the left wall. The Trailsman intended to be standing at the crack when Bubba Jones came through it. Soon, lightning flashes lit up the narrow crack for him to see. Fargo dismounted and flattened his back to one side of it. Then he listened for what would bring Bubba out, the noisy sounds of the wagons.

After a lengthy wait, he heard the wagons coming and got ready. Then he heard the boys working their way down inside the split. They were laughing, making smart remarks, and playing harmonicas. One from higher up called Bubba by name. Farther down, Bubba answered. Fargo heard a rock clatter down the crack and splash into the mud at his feet. Bubba Jones would appear any second now. Fargo made a fist and cocked it.

Bubba stepped out of the split. Fargo powered the fist into his nose and mouth. Bubba Jones dropped like a two-hundred-pound bag of potatoes. Holding his nose, Fargo drew his Colt and fired one shot into the clouds. That's all it took to send the rest of the good ol' boys on their way back up the fissure. Fargo propped Bubba's unconscious body against the wall and left him there to wake up and wonder what had hit him. God, the man stunk.

Moments later, Fargo rejoined the wagons. They proceeded unhindered to the other mouth of Trouble Canyon. The rain ceased when they were well in Snake Valley. Fargo rode to the tart wagon to check on the women. All but Can Can, who held the reins, were huddled beneath the canvas. Fargo rode to Blinky's wagon and asked him how much farther to Deadly Canyon. Blinky told him less than two miles.

"How long is Deadly Canyon, Blinky?" Fargo asked, a trace of urgency in his voice. He hoped to hear "short," because he wanted it done and over quickly.

Blinky answered, "Deadly is the shortest of them all."

"Good," Fargo replied.

"And one of the roughest," Blinky added.

"What do you mean by roughest? The terrain or the Chinamen?"

"Both. We've never gotten past the leaping Chinese. That's because the canyon is so narrow. They can hear us coming when we enter it. There's no telling where they will leap from. There's a lot of boulders in the canyon. Lot of gulleys for 'em to hide in, too."

"Not to worry, Blinky. I know where to find their crack. I'll be there waiting for them to spill out. Then I'll do to them what I did to Bubba Jones."

"Oh? And where might that crack be?"

"There are four blue spruce. One is dead. The crack is behind it."

"Fargo, there ain't no blue spruces, dead or alive, in that canyon. Who told you that? Dan McGrew? If he did, he lied."

"Aw, shit," Fargo muttered. He took a deep breath, sighed and confessed, "No. Chief Crossed-Eyes told me."

Blinky chuckled. "You cain't believe a word that old buzzard says. As a matter of fact, there ain't no trees of any kind in the canyon. However, there are plenty of cracks on both sides. And all of 'em go to the top."

Fargo now knew he had a problem. The attack could come from anywhere at any time. Moreover, the Chinese would not necessarily use the same crack. He asked Blinky, "How many Chinamen are there?"

"Six, plus the one with the gong. He don't leap or fight."

Fargo groaned and rode ahead. The lightning quit flashing. The thunder stopped rumbling. The air grew still and turned cold. When Fargo reached the narrow mouth of Deadly Canyon, a light snow began to fall. "That's all I need," the big man mumbled. "Snow. With my current run of bad luck, I'll get stuck in Blood Gorge. Cooped up with Charleen Bodner, I'll have to listen to her bitch till the spring thaw. Aaugh!"

The Ovaro knickered lowly, as though he agreed.

Fargo halted just inside the entrance to wait for the tart wagon. Sitting easy in the saddle, he told himself he would protect as many of the females as he could. That's when he heard the gong. The final leg of the game had begun.

As Blinky's wagon rumbled past him, Fargo told him not to stop regardless of what happened. "Just keep your forward progress, Blinky. I'll be driving the tart wagon." He told O'Malley the same thing when the Irishman passed him. Then Fargo stepped from his horse onto the floorboard of the tart wagon and took the reins from Can Can. He motioned for her to get under the canvas with the other women. She was quick to obey. Then Fargo waited and watched, waited and watched some more. He was sure Blinky had passed the halfway point, and the Chinamen had not yet leapt. Time passed, and they still had not appeared. Were it not for the slow, measured beating of the gong to say otherwise, Fargo was ready to believe the snow muted the sounds of the wagons to the point that the Chinamen couldn't get a fix on them.

He saw the vague outlines of the mouth of the canyon. His hopes soared. It appeared the wagons would get through.

Then one of the women sneezed. She sneezed loud enough to wake the dead, loud enough to make Fargo flinch. She sneezed a second time. Fargo held his breath. Blinky made it through the maw. Then O'Malley did, too.

Then six black-clad forms leapt onto the tart wagon. They slashed the snow with the sides of their hands and went "Aahyee!"

Fargo glanced over his shoulder and saw two spin and kick backward. The women started screaming. The black-clad forms paused, became tense, and looked at one another.

Fargo fell backward off the seat and onto the canvas. He did a backward flip and landed on his feet. He grabbed and started throwing the black-clad forms out of the wagon into the snow. One kicked him in the mouth. Another jabbed his fingers in Fargo's abdomen. Two vaulted over the side of the wagon. Fargo couldn't get rid of them. The team had halted. The gong beater appeared at the right side of the wagon. Fargo was grabbing and flinging black-clad forms as fast as he could. The sheet of canvas was yanked off the shrieking females. The gong beater shouted something in Chinese. Instantly all the black-clad forms froze and held their stances.

The gong beater removed his black hood. Fa-ting smiled up at Fargo and said, "Fa-go, what you do by and by these I'shmen?"

The game had finally ended.

Fargo relaxed.

11

Fa-ting rode next to Fargo in the driver's seat. They reminisced while following Blinky and O'Malley down the narrow, breathtaking switchbacks that led to Blood Gorge and the Shamrock.

"Why did you leave Carson Valley, Fa-ting?" Fargo inquired.

"Too much shoot-em, Fa-go. Ma-goo and bagpipe came by cook shack. We follow Ma-goo this place. Ma-goo teach how play game. Chinese play good. No?"

Fargo nodded. "Did you see Missy Hilary before you left?"

"Missy Hilary and Madam Margot make whole lot money. They velly lich now."

And so it went during the steep, dangerous decent. Near the bottom the snow stopped falling. The morning sun filtered through the overcast and gave Fargo a glimpse of the Shamrock. Smoke came out two chimneys, promising warmth inside. Snow covered everything, the trees, the Shamrock, and the entire gorge. Fargo asked the location of Miss Precious Goodbody's Golden Gully.

Fa-ting pointed to a shack a short distance from the Shamrock. "Look up, Fa-go. You see big black hole." He went on to say the hole was across the gully from where the shack stood. "Dat shack hold I'shman's gold. Plenty lot gold, Fa-go. They lich."

Fargo nodded. He wondered if they had it assayed. From the size of the shack and Fa-ting's implication that it held a considerable amount, Fargo concluded they were rich, indeed. He negotiated the final switchback and drove on level ground to the Shamrock.

The females hurried inside. The Irishmen each toted two kegs and followed them. The Chinamen also carried two kegs inside. Fargo led the Ovaro behind the Shamrock, where he had seen a wide shed open on one side. In the shed he found two burros and enough hay and oats to last them and the teams all winter. He relieved the stallion of his burden, then let him eat hay.

Fargo entered the Shamrock through the back door. A spacious kitchen and potbellied man kneading dough greeted him. Fargo introduced himself.

The fellow replied, "They call me Tubby. Jeremiah is my real name. Jeremiah O'Malley. Me and Trevor are cousins. Hand me that pan, willya? The big one. I'm fixing breakfast. Miss Precious likes biscuits with her breakfast, so I'm making some. You a miner? Don't look like one."

"Not a miner."

"Cowboy, then?"

"Neither am I a cowpoke."

"Well, what are you?"

"A trailsman."

"Never heard of such. Them underclothes are dripping wet. Go inside and stand by the fire. I don't have time to stand here and jaw with you, anyhow."

Fargo stepped through the only door in the kitchen. A great room—he estimated its size would be at least fifty feet square—lay before him. The bare rafters of the roof were two stories high. A narrow staircase with handrails on one side went up to the balcony on the second level. The staircase butted an outer wall. Wide planks were used to make the floor. Rugs lit-

tered the floor. A piano stood against the wall opposite the staircase. The bar ended short of the stairs.
Candles spaced two feet apart lined the walls. Several
lamps stood on the shelf behind the bar. Rustic, Fargo
thought.

All the Ute and miners were in the room. He
counted eighty people. The women had their fannies
to the fire that blazed in the unusually wide hearth.
Miss Precious was nowhere in sight. Through a front
window Fargo saw the kegs had already been off-loaded
and divided in piles.

Fargo stepped behind the bar and poured himself a
shot of Irish whiskey. As he raised the shot glass to his
lips, a movement on the balcony drew his attention.
Glancing up, he saw a statuesque attractive female
standing at the railing. She smiled down at him. He
toasted her with the shot glass.

Grace had apparently seen the gesture. She stepped
away from the hearth. She looked up. Wide-eyed, she
gasped, "Auggie? Is . . . is . . . that you?" Then she
shrieked, "Oh, yes! You are really Auggie Harlow.
I've found my Auggie."

As she ran up the stairs, Auggie ran down them.
They met open-armed, hugged and kissed, shrieked
and giggled. Everyone watched the two women come
down the stairs arm in arm and go to the bar across
from where Fargo stood. Grace beamed as she said,
"Fargo, darling, I want you to meet my best friend,
Auggie Harlow."

Fargo touched the brim of his hat. Auggie offered
her hand to him. He kissed the back of it. Their eyes
met and locked. He saw the irises of her eyes were
the same color as his. She also had black hair like
him, though much longer than his. Auggie had a
heart-shaped face dominated by a wide mouth having
full lips. The corners were upturned, giving her a per-
petual naughty grin. Full breasts gave way to a slightly

rounded tummy, which accented nice hips. He reckoned she had shapely buttocks, too, and long legs. In a word, Auggie Harlow, by any name, was desirable. He said, "Pardon my lack of clothing, but I—"

"You have a beautiful body, Mr. Fargo," Auggie interrupted. "I see naked men all the time. Don't apologize."

Auggie turned and hopped up to sit on the bartop. She whistled through her teeth to gain everyone's attention, then said, "No mine work today, boys. I'm declaring a holiday. We'll celebrate the arrival of Grace Hatfield and these adorable French tarts she whispered in my ear about. Ooompapa, you and the rest of the Achtungers fetch the whiskey. Let's get drunk and have fun."

"I'll drink to that," Chief Crossed-Eyes hollered.

The achtungers went to get the kegs. They ooompapahed all the way.

An Irishman stepped to the piano. He began playing a lively tune. The Scottish drummer and fifers picked up on it after a few bars, then the bagpipers did, too. Miners grabbed the tarts and twins, swung them away from the hearth, and launched into a fast foot-stomping jig.

Auggie swung her legs up over the bar and hooked them around Fargo's neck. She purred, "Big man, I will teach you many tricks this winter. That's a promise. But not today. Grace and I have lots of catching up to do."

"I leave at dawn, ma'am," he replied.

"Oh? What a pity. What a loss." She released him slowly.

He lifted her off the bar and kissed her open-mouthed. He felt her tremble as she moaned, "Oh, God . . . you do taste good." Her arms curled around his neck. She pressed her lips tightly to his and began lolling her head, probing with her hot tongue.

Grace coughed discreetly and broke their kiss.

Auggie whispered, "We'll finish what you started later, big man."

Fargo nodded. He moved to the hearth to lower his temperature.

As the day wore on and the shadows lengthened in the gorge, the frivolity at the Shamrock increased in tempo. Everyone was in a joyous, carefree mood. Clothes were shed. The tarts put on a show. The miners clapped in time with the music as the tarts shimmied and shook.

Miss Precious stood on the bar and stripped. Two candles were lit and put on the bar. The room became quiet. Nobody moved. From the soft glow of the candle's light, everyone watched Miss Precious' nicely shaped hips begin to sway. She dropped a silver dollar on the bar, parted her feet, squatted, wiggled her bottom, then rose quickly. The silver dollar was gone. She parted her silky thighs and the coin fell onto the bar. She shot a wink to Fargo, then turned and bent at the waist. The crowd moaned as the bushy black fluff of pubic hair appeared. The middle finger of her right hand briefly rubbed the fluff, then disappeared in it. The finger moved away. She straightened and looked over her shoulder. Holding the erotic pose, she began tensing and relaxing her buttock cheek muscles, one after the other. The movement of her cheeks in the soft glow mesmerized all in the room.

The front door swung open and brought the sultry exhibition to an abrupt halt. All eyes kicked toward the door. Miss Comely walked in, then Lay-Me-Down, followed by Gold Pan, the banker, and Tops.

Miss Comely spied Grace right off. The old whore stiffened, gasped, "Oh, no, not the Bible-thumping crusader!"

Grace lowered her gaze, mumbled apologetically,

"I'm not a crusader anymore, Miss Comely. I'm a fallen woman like you."

"What are you people doing here?" Miss Precious wanted to know.

Miss Comely approached the bar. Looking up at her, she explained, "That woman"—she nodded toward Grace—"ran me out of business over in Powderhorn. Lay-Me-Down, here"—she nodded toward the skinny Ute saloon girl—"said her chief knew miners who would put up the cash for us to tough out the winter and finish the new saloon next spring. So we went to her tribe to talk to the chief. Lay-Me-Down's people told us the chief was away, playing the game. They told us where to find this place, that maybe he would be here. Is he?"

Miss Precious looked at and nodded toward the old man sitting cross-legged, well into his cups. "That's Chief Crossed-Eyes over there," she said.

Crossed-Eyes called over to Miss Comely, "How much wampum do you need?"

"Wampum?" Miss Comely answered. "I don't need wampum. I need cash."

"Will gold do?" Miss Precious asked. "If so, how much?"

"Hell, I don't know. About two thousand dollars' worth, I guess."

"You got it," Miss Precious announced. "Tubby will bag and have it ready for you to take tomorrow morning. Meanwhile, you interrupted our party. You are welcome to join in on the drinking and dancing. Gink, start playing your piano. The celebration goes on."

The party-goers quickly picked up where their joviality had left off.

Much later Fargo watched Auggie and Grace drift toward the stairs and finally go up them. They were laughing when they disappeared in the dark hallway on the second level. He presumed they would talk the night away.

A twin's voice spoke from the shadows left of where Fargo stood at the hearth. Before turning to face her, he decided she was Maureen, for the voice cooed to him, "Fargo, darling, I need you." She stepped out of the shadows and smiled naughtily at him. Her hands each cupped a breast. Maureen started massaging them and moaned, "I need you now."

Maureen was now rubbing her belly and fiery-red strawberry-colored patch. Her eyelids drooped, her lips parted. Her wet tongue glistened in the firelight as she licked all around her lips. She came to him slowly and pressed her nakedness to him. She curled one hand on his nape, the other dipped to and fondled his crotch. Kissing his throat, she whispered, "Take me now, Fargo, darling." Her hot breath caressed his left ear.

Fargo cradled the hot-blooded filly in his strong arms and carried her upstairs to the darkened hallway. She made little love sounds and nibbled his ear and cheeks while he looked for a door that stood ajar. "Hurry, darling. I'm so hot I'm coming already," she purred in his ear.

He finally found a door partway open and nudged it full open with a boot. Moonlight spilled through the room's one window and bathed the bed in its diffused glow. He lowered her onto the bed, then started to remove his gun belt.

Maureen rolled onto her back. Quick as a wink she had his fly open and pulled out his throbbing shaft. She looked up into his eyes, then at it. Then she tilted her head to ride down the edge of the bed and opened her mouth to take in his manhood. She fed the head in, paused to swish her hot, moist tongue all over it, then took in about half and started sucking. When Fargo pulled back far enough to withdraw completely, her tightened lips smacked. She lay there breathing rapidly, mewing childlike, and looking up at him.

Fargo took off the gun belt and put his Colt under the pillow. He undressed, then sat on the bed to remove the calf sheath and pull off his boots. Maureen waited to hear the stiletto and sheath thud on the floor, but the hellcat didn't wait to hear the boots hit the floor. She bent around him and fed his member between her lips. When Fargo reclined and raised his legs onto the bed, she followed his every move while she bobbed her head and continued to suck. Taking a breather, she whispered hotly, lovingly, "Darling, you're so well-endowed that it makes my jaws hurt."

"Then we should try your lower lips and let your jaws rest," he muttered.

She lay on top of him. Fargo's organ parted her silky-smooth thighs. She worked its hard length to ride between her hot lower lips, then started hunching on it, making it glide up and down the length of her juicy slit. Fargo took in a mouthful of her left breast and began tongue-massaging it.

Maureen gasped, "Oh, me . . . oh, my . . . so good, so good. Nice, nice . . . get the other one, too."

He slipped over and sucked the right nipple. She pressed down, gasped, "Bite me . . . oh, God, yes . . . bite me." Maureen started whimpering.

Fargo love-bit the nipple, then captured all the pillowy mound his mouth could hold. Her head lolled and she writhed. She rolled off him and got on her hands and knees. Gulping, she looked at him and said, "I want to feel it like this."

He got behind her and spread her knees with his. She put her head on the pillow and grabbed two of the iron bars on the headboard. He looked down at the strawberry patch, positioned his blood-swollen summit for entry, took her by the hips, and pulled them to him just far enough to work the crown in and let her get a feel for what was to follow.

She gasped, "Jesus, Jesus . . . darling . . . you're so large . . . so big."

He thrust and went in about halfway, then began to gyrate slowly.

Maureen moaned her pleasure. "Oh, my God, does that ever feel so good to me. Don't stop, don't ever stop."

He watched her hands grip tighter around the bars, foretelling what he knew she was about to do. Accordingly, he relaxed his hold on her hips. Maureen pushed back as hard as she could and screamed between clenched teeth, "Aaugh! Oh, my God! Jesus, Jesus, you're long and big."

Fargo still had about an inch to go. He tightened his grip on her hips and gave all of it to her.

Maureen murmured, "More . . . harder . . . go faster. Don't stop. Please, don't stop." She began trying to twist the bars into knots. She buried her face in the pillow and met Fargo's every thrust with one of her own.

Her contractions came without any warning. She was as surprised as Fargo. He shoved in as deeply as he could, then waited for them to bring about his eruption. When it came, she gasped, "Flood me, Fargo . . . that's it, darling . . . fill me with your hotness." She collapsed onto her stomach and lay there trembling and taking quick breaths.

Fargo reached for a towel and dampened it in the porcelain bowl of water on the nightstand next to the bed. He cleaned himself, then tucked the towel between Maureen's thighs. After a long moment she turned on her left side. Maureen's breathing had slowed but her eyes had not. They roamed to various parts of his body, paused now and then, then moved on. Fargo wondered what was on her mind. Listening

159

to the laughter coming from the great room? The piano? Perhaps both, he decided. He saw the beginning of a smile form on her mouth. It vanished as quickly as it had appeared. He lifted his gaze.

Maureen asked, "What are you thinking?"

"What are you?"

"How wonderful I feel. How satisfied. And . . ."

He waited for her to finish the sentence. When it became obvious she let it trail off intentionally to pique his curiosity to the point that he would drag it out of her, he refused to accommodate her and remained silent.

Maureen rolled onto her back. Cleaning up, she finished what she started to say. In a near whisper she said, "I've changed my mind about staying here for the winter. I want to go to Tucson with you."

"Oh? Have you discussed this change with Charleen?" Even though he doubted she had, he sought verification.

"No. She wouldn't go, anyhow. Staying here was her idea. She would only cause trouble for you if she went. Bitching and griping, mostly. Charleen can be a royal pain in the ass."

Fargo could agree to that. He nodded.

Maureen propped on one elbow and looked at him for a long moment. Then she hit with another bombshell. "Frankly, I'm tired of Charleen. I want to leave her behind. Start fresh. Make a new life for myself . . . and you."

Here it comes, he thought. Altar talk. And he wasn't completely mistaken.

When he made no reply, Maureen apparently took it as a sign of encouragement and hit him with another bombshell. "Let me take care of you, darling. I have the means, and money, to do it. We will live comfortably. You'll see. Charleen would only be in the way.

You wouldn't have to work. You could stop being a trailsman and stay at home with me."

That does it, he said inwardly, and tensed at the mere thought of her idea. Maureen was crowding him, and Fargo didn't like it. The only thing that stopped him from speaking his mind, which he was about to do, was the commencement of a loud brawl downstairs.

Maureen bolted up. Staring at the door, she asked, "My God, what's all that racket? It sounds as though the miners are killing one another."

"Probably so." He left the bed and told her to come watch with him from the balcony.

At the railing they looked down on a first-class melee. Fists were flying all around the room, hitting faces and heads too numb from Irish whiskey to cause much pain.

Fools Gold climbed atop the bar, then dived onto Oden's back. O'Malley, no longer a coward, pummeled Dangerous Dan McGrew's big head. Fargo watched Ooompapa knock a rogue halfway across the room, then himself absorb a hard blow to the gut. It went on and on until one man, Blue-blackbeard, remained standing, and he was a bloody mess, as was the floor and the miners sprawled on it. Blue-blackbeard staggered to claim his prize: Ooolala and Can Can. Fargo scanned the room. He didn't see Charleen.

With arms around their waists, Fargo and Maureen strolled back to the room and lay on the bed. Maureen didn't pick up on her earlier line of thought. Fargo was thankful for that. Neither did she make a secondary move at lovemaking on him, like he fully expected her to do. So many did. To the contrary, Maureen snuggled up to him and went to sleep.

Fargo listened to the silence for a while, then closed his eyes, and he, too, found sleep came easy.

An explosion that shook the bed and rattled the

windowpanes jarred Fargo's eyes open and sent his gun hand beneath the pillow to grasp the Colt's handle. He brought the weapon up with him as he sat. His eyes focused on the window momentarily before he thought it odd the explosion hadn't awakened Maureen. His free hand reached to shake her awake . . . and she wasn't there, nor anywhere else in the room.

Fargo got dressed in record-setting time. He flung the door open, ran down the hall, took the stairs four at a time, and saw Maureen in the crowd flocking out the door. He bulled his way outside and grabbed her arm. She wrenched free and ran with the miners heading for the shack. Fargo didn't try to catch her a second time. He slowed his pace and watched the massive cloud of gold dust glittering in the morning's early light as it fell slowly back to earth.

Out of the debris of the demolished shack crawled the other twin. The twins' saddled horses and burdened jenny stood nearby, ready in all respects for the trail. Maureen rushed up to her twin and spat, "My God, Maureen, can't you do anything right? I told you blackpowder wasn't necessary."

Fools Gold was beside himself. Pivoting on one foot and flapping his arms, he looked into the sparkling cloud and shouted angrily, "You, you, bitch, you! Three years' work and you've blown it to kingdom come."

Gold Pan caught a handful of the falling dust. He fingered it, frowned, then looked at the Irishman and said, "Gold dust it ain't. Iron pirite it is. Fools Gold, you boys have been digging for worthless fool's gold." He brushed his hands.

Fargo turned to the banker, Samuel B. Quick, and said, "You will find your bank's money in one of the bags on their jenny. As a matter of fact, you will find more than you lost. I suspect the twins have been stealing their way across the country." Fargo looked at Charleen and asked, "Am I not correct?"

"Yes," she quipped bitterly.

"And you wanted to give me the good life," Fargo mused aloud. As he shook his head, he chuckled.

Chief Crossed-Eyes staggered through the crowd and braced himself on Fargo. He mumbled drunkenly, "Paleface, is the game over?"

Fargo answered through an easy grin, "No, but the twins' game is up."

Crossed-Eyes blinked, asked, "What do you mean by that? Huh, paleface?"

Shaking his head, Fargo smiled. The old chief would never understand. He turned the old man around, aimed him at the Shamrock, and said, "Go find Lay-Me-Down. She will tell you."

Crossed-Eyes staggered toward the Shamrock. The miners drifted with him. Quick started removing the bags from the jenny. The twins held each other close as they walked back to the two-story structure. Tears streamed down Charleen's face when she glanced over her shoulder for a last look at the bags. Fargo picked up a shovel and walked to the mine.

He easily spotted the mound of leavings the Irishmen had excavated from the mine. He dug through the thin layer of snow and dumped a shovelful of the leavings on the mound. As expected, he saw much blue mixed in with the soil and pieces of rock. He smiled as he pushed the shovel into the leavings and left it there.

Fargo went to the shed and made the Ovaro trail-ready, then led him to the Shamrock's front door. He stepped to the bar to have a final shot of good Irish whiskey. Miss Precious poured it for him. He tossed it down, then shot her a wink and said, "If I were you, I'd have the mine's leavings assayed soon."

"Why? It's nothing but dirt, pebbles, and blue stuff."

"Take my advice and have it assayed, anyhow."

Miss Precious followed him outside and watched him mount up and head toward the rising sun.

Fargo looked behind and saw her walking toward the shovel. He muttered to his stallion, "She's got enough silver in the leavings to buy Denver."

The Ovaro nodded. A knicker rumbled from his throat.

Fargo rode out of Blood Gorge and put the sun on his left.

LOOKING FORWARD!

**The following is the opening
section from the next novel in the exciting
Trailsman series from Signet:**

THE TRAILSMAN #116
KANSAS KILL

*The Kansas Territory, 1861,
where the Smokey Hills cast a long shadow,
and human greed an even longer one. . . .*

He wasn't afraid. But he was nervous. There was no question about that, Doc Schubert admitted as he dried his freshly scrubbed hands and slipped into the long white laboratory gown. He tied the gown around his long, lanky figure and drew a deep breath. He hadn't done this kind of operation in years. In Clay Springs it was mostly broken bones and bullet wounds. Lottie, his nurse and companion for fifteen years, had just given the last dose of chloroform to the man stretched out on the operating table. Tom Johnson was not only one of the wealthiest ranchers in the region but an old friend, and Doc Schubert was determined to do the best his skills would let him.

Lottie waited, ready with cotton swabs, instruments, and bandages. Doc Schubert paused beside the table to glance at Alicia Johnson, clad in the white medical gown. Tom Johnson's wife, and some thirty years his junior, Alicia had insisted on being there. "You never know when you'll need an extra hand," she had said, and everyone knew how devoted she was to Tom. So he had agreed and given Alicia an afternoon of intensive instruction. She nodded to him now, standing back a few feet beside the table of extra bandages and extra basins of water. Doc Schubert returned the nod, paused beside the prostrate figure on the table, and picked up the scalpel from the instrument tray. He drew a deep breath and leaned forward.

His hand was steady, a reassuring feeling, as he made the first incision down Tom Johnson's belly. He felt Alicia Johnson flinch, cast a quick stare at her, and saw that she was all right and under control. Lottie reached forward with a clamp and sponges as he widened the incision. He worked quickly, pleased to feel the old deftness returning. Doc Schubert smiled. It was going well. He was just about to begin the critical phase of the operation when he heard the front door burst open. He whirled to stare at the three men who rushed into the house, all with drawn guns.

"Get out of here," he shouted. "I'm in the middle of an operation." But the three men strode forward, the tallest one in front. "I've no money here. Get out," Doc Schubert shouted again. The tallest man brushed past him to halt beside the operating table. He fired three shots, and Tom Johnson's opened, helpless body jerked convulsively as the bullets slammed into it. "Jesus," Doc Schubert swore as he dived forward and grabbed the man around the waist. But as he did, he heard the others open fire. He saw Lottie's white become red as bullets tore into her just before he felt the exploding, searing pain in his back as two shots struck him.

The man tore from his grasp as he fell forward, and

Doc Schubert felt the pain consuming him, welling up through his body, engulfing all else. He fell to one knee, and in his last moments of consciousness, he saw Alicia Johnson turn to flee when another shot rang out and she went down. Doc Schubert, his face contorted with excruciating pain, managed to gasp out a single word as the tall man stood over him. "Why?" he rasped and pitched forward to the floor. His long, lanky body shuddered out its last breath and lay still.

The lights were burning brightly in the distant house, the big man noted as he rode slowly through the first lavender touch of twilight. Sitting casually astride the magnificent Ovaro with its glistening black fore- and hind-quarters and gleaming, pure-white midsection, the big man thought of how many years it had been since he last saw Doc Schubert. Skye Fargo smiled as the warm remembrances flowed through him. He and Doc had combined their efforts to bring in a wagon train riddled with sickness and Cheyenne arrows. It had been weeks of sweat, hard work and death waiting at every turn, the kind of effort that brings men together in a special bond.

When it was over, he'd seen the doc safely back to Clay Springs and stayed on himself for a spell. And now, with too many years in between, he'd finished a job near enough to Clay Springs for a surprise visit to Doc. He'd passed through town and he still had a few hundred yards to go when he saw the three men rush from the house and vault onto waiting horses. Fargo felt the frown dig into his brow as the three men raced away. Something more than apprehension instantly stabbed into him and he put the pinto into a gallop. The three riders were almost out of sight in the gathering dusk as they raced across the almost treeless flat land. He reached the house and skidded to a halt. Maybe Doc had sent the trio racing off on a mission, perhaps to bring back some special serum, Fargo murmured as he leapt to the ground. But the stabbing apprenension inside him told him that the thought was more hope than probability. He strode through the half-opened door, one hand on the butt of the big Colt at his hip.

Only silence greeted him as he stepped through the vestibule and into the next room, where he felt an oath stick in his throat. "God almighty," he breathed, his eyes sweeping the terrible scene spread out in front of him. Blood poured from the body on the operating table, not only from the incision opened in his abdomen but from the three gaping bullet holes in his chest. Fargo's eyes went to the floor, where Doc Schubert lay in a widening circle of blood. He knelt down, pressed his fingers into the doc's neck to feel for a pulse. There was none and he cursed silently as he lifted to his gaze. Lottie, Doc's nurse, lay at the head of the operating table in a lab coat that had once been white but was now almost entirely red.

He rose, stared down at the carnage, his lake-blue eyes narrowed as they took in every detail. He was about to leave when he heard the soft moan. The sound came from the adjoining room and he rushed in on one long stride to see the woman on the floor, one hand holding the back of her calf. She stared at him with wide brown eyes that were a combination of hope and fear. "Jesus, you're alive," Fargo said as he dropped to one knee beside her.

"Yes." She nodded. "I went down and they thought they'd killed me like they did the others."

Fargo moved her hand and saw the thin line of red running down a nicely turned calf. 'The bullet passed through the fleshy part of your leg, but you'll still need it treated," he said, and paused to take in the woman. Between thirty and thirty-five, he guessed, a face a shade heavy but still very attractive, brown eyes that appraised with the look of someone who had seen enough of the world, brown hair with a hint of red in it, and full lips on a wide mouth. A face that just avoided hardness, he decided. "What happened here?" he asked.

"Three men, looking to rob Doc Schubert, I guess. They just came in and started shooting," she said.

"What were you doing here?" Fargo questioned.

"I'm Alicia Johnson. The man on the operating table was my husband," she said.

"Jesus, I'm sorry," Fargo murmured, and rose to his feet, reached out, and lifted the woman onto a blue settee. "You'll be more comfortable on this," he said.

"There's a young doctor in Hillsdale, about five miles east. Maybe you could fetch him. I don't think I could ride," Alicia Johnson said. "Who are you, mister?" she asked.

"Fargo . . . Skye Fargo. I'm an old friend of Doc Schubert's. I came ready to pay him a surprise visit," Fargo said, and heard the bitter anger come into his voice.

"Skye Fargo? The one they call the Trailsman?" Alicia Johnson asked, and he nodded. "Tom and Doc Schubert were good friends and I've heard Doc talk about you."

"If I'd been five minutes earlier this wouldn't have happened," Fargo bit out. "You've a sheriff in Clay Springs?"

"No, but Jack Hook is the undertaker and unofficial mayor. Get hold of him," Alicia Johnson said.

"I'll fetch the doc for you first," Fargo said.

"Yes, please," she said.

"Then I'm going to track down those three murdering bastards," Fargo said, his voice hardening.

Alicia Johnson's brown eyes stayed on him. "Maybe I can help you with that," she said. "We'll talk after you get back."

Fargo nodded, spun on his heel, and strode into the adjoining room and past the scene of vicious death. Besides, he had already taken note of everything he needed to see.

Night had fallen when he rode the Ovaro east at a fast trot, letting the horse's powerful stride devour the relatively flat terrain. Not far away, the Smokey Hills rose up in rolling outline under a half-moon. He finally reached the town of Hillside, which turned out to be small, most of it warehouses and shops with but a few houses. He found someone who directed him to Doc Dawson's house, where he found a young man who was visibly shaken at what he heard.

"My God, Doc Schubert. He's been a real good friend since I came out here," the young man said, his voice quavering. "I'll get my rig. That way I can drive Alicia home."

"Good," Fargo said, and watched the younger man hurry to a small barn behind the house, to reappear soon after driving a doctor's buggy with the high, overhanging roof and canework on the lower portion of the body. Fargo fell in beside him.

"Did you know Tom Johnson, too?" Doc Dawson asked as they moved through the night.

"No, just Doc Schubert," Fargo replied.

"Tom Johnson was well-liked and one of the richest ranchers in the region," the younger man said.

"From my quick look at him on the operating table I'd say he was pushing sixty," Fargo commented.

"Maybe a little more," Doc Dawson said. "He married Alicia five years sgo, after his first wife, Vera, died. God, Alicia's lucky to be alive."

"Damn lucky," Fargo said. "But they won't get away with it."

"Hell, I'd say they have already. They're gone. God knows where," Doc Dawson said.

"They left a trail. Come morning, I'll pick it up. I'll get them," Fargo said, and his voice was a grim promise.

The big, old house finally came into sight, lights burning brightly. As they reached it, Fargo saw a lone horse tethered outside. He held up one hand as he slid from the saddle. "Stay behind me," he said as the younger man swung from the wagon. Fargo entered the house with the Colt in hand, raised and ready to fire. He moved through the terrible scene and into the adjoining room. Alicia Johnson was still on the settee, her one leg resting stretched out, but she had company. A young woman turned as he entered and he saw the tearstains still on high cheekbones.

"It's him, the man I told you came in," Fargo heard Alicia say, and the young woman's face relaxed. Fargo saw Doc Dawson hurry past him, his little black bag in one hand, and go to Alicia.

"I'm Ellen Johnson," the young woman said, words coming with an effort. "I came by to see how Dad's operation had gone and found . . ." she said, her voice trailing off as she turned away. Fargo waited as she composed herself and watched the doctor treat Alicia Johnson's calf wound. Ellen Johnson turned back to him and he took in an attractive face, perhaps a little long, with a straight nose, thin but nicely shaped lips. He saw light-blue eyes and very black hair cut short with long, very black narrow eyebrows to match. A long neck moved down to a narrow figure with breasts that flowed in a long, curving line under a white shirt. He guessed Ellen Johnson to be in her early twenties. "You were coming to visit Doc Schubert, Alicia told me," she said.

"That's right, and I'm going to get the stinking bastards who did this," Fargo said. A quick glance at Alica Johnson saw that the doc had her calf tightly bandaged and was helping her to stand.

"You'll be able to walk fine in a day or two, but keep the bandage on till I come see you," Doc Dawson told Alicia. The woman had taken off the long white laboratory coat, and Fargo saw a full figure, perhaps ten pounds too much on it, but she carried it well. Her breasts had no sag in them, her wide hips and strong full thighs pressed against a black skirt. There was a ripe sensuousness to Alicia Johnson, he decided.

"You had something to tell me," Fargo reminded the woman.

"Yes. I know where they were going," she said. Fargo felt his brows lift in surprise. "To Rock Station," Alicia Johnson said. "One of them, the tall one, said so. He has a sandy mustache and a scar on his lower lip."

"How'd he come to say so?" Fargo questioned.

"I heard him tell the others they'd meet there. I guess they intended to separate," Alicia said.

"That's smart thinking on their part," Doc Dawson put in, and Fargo nodded agreement. "I'll take Alicia back to the ranch now," the doctor said.

Fargo glanced at Ellen Johnson. "You go with

them. There's nothing you can do here except take in more pain," he said.

"I don't live at the ranch. I've my own place," Ellen Johnson said, a flash of pointedness in her tone.

"I'll see you home," Fargo said.

"Thanks, but I'll be all right. You go on. Getting those murdering killers comes first," she said.

"Rock Station's a full day's ride. I've plenty of time. I'll see you back," Fargo said.

The young woman drew a deep sigh. "All right. I'd really appreciate that. I'm feeling pretty shaky," she said. She walked through the other room with her eyes staring straight ahead, and Fargo followed but hung back a moment to sweep the terrible scene again with a quick but penetrating glance. His mouth was a thin line when he strode outside.

Alicia was in the doctor's buggy as he paused. Her brown eyes sought him out. "You'll come back and tell me, won't you? I won't be sleeping much till I know they've paid for this," she said.

"Count on it," Fargo said, and Alicia let gratefulness pass through her full-cheeked face. Doc Dawson rolled the buggy forward and Fargo climbed onto the Ovaro and swung alongside Ellen Johnson's light bay. He rode beside her as she followed the buggy for some quarter-mile and then cut west from the road. He rode in silence with her and heard her struggle with sobs until she finally gained back at least surface composure. "You were close to your pa," he remarked softly.

"Very," Ellen Johnson said.

"How long since you moved from your pa's ranch?" Fargo asked.

"Since Alicia moved in," Ellen said, fell silent for

a moment, and threw him a sharp, sidelong glance. "And I know what you're thinking," she said.

"And what would that be?" he asked.

"Daughter resents new wife," she snapped.

"It happens often enough."

"I suppose it does."

"Then sometimes people just don't get along together," Fargo said.

"And sometimes there's a lot more," Ellen said as she led him through a line of silver maple to a modest ranch house with three corrals and a barn spread out behind it. "Home, sweet home," she said, and dismounted in front of the house. "Thanks for seeing me back."

"My pleasure," Fargo said.

"I'd invite you in, but I know you want to get on your way and I don't feel much like playing hostess," Ellen said. There was a direct frankness to her, very likable in its own way, he decided. "You told Alicia you'd be back to tell her you settled accounts. Would it be too much to ask you to stop by here?"

"I planned to do that, especially as how there's something strange about this whole thing," Fargo said.

"Something strange?" Ellen Johnson frowned. "Because it was so vicious?"

"It was that, but I've seen vicious before. There was something else."

The young woman's frown deepened. "Such as?" she pressed.

"I don't know, not yet. Maybe I'll have some answers when I get back," Fargo said.

"Be careful. I wouldn't want to see you as their fourth victim," Ellen Johnson said.

"Me neither," Fargo said with a wry grin as he wheeled the horse around. He left her frowning after him, a slender, lovely figure that combined pain and lonely strength. He put the pinto into a steady trot northeast, his thoughts already turned to the task ahead. An apparant random robbery attempt that turned into three vicious murders. Only maybe there had been nothing random at all. There had been little things. He had picked them up. His trailsman's eye always searched for the little things. Sometimes they were unimportant. Sometimes they meant everything. He was going to find out about these. Doc Schubert deserved that.